Acknowledgement

I would like to dedicate this collection of stories, poems and illustrations to all of the people who have helped and believed in me along the way. A huge thank you to all of those folk who helped bring this collection of stories and poems to fruition. With particular thanks to Bronwen Burgess, Carmit Kordov and Jayne Howes for their editing skills, assistance and patience.

Works by the same author

"The Man Behind the Glass" (2015) ISBN:9780995609600

"The Maidenswell Folly" (2017) ISBN:9780995609617

"The Movement of Light" (2018) ISBN:9780995609624

A Sense of the Other
and other Strange Tales

Written and illustrated by Greg Howes

Foreword

All things became much more terrible and far more beautiful at once. A dragonfly emerging, wings a-glisten, from years of safe harbour below a dense and watery film.

Chapter	Name	Page No

Other Stories and Poems within this volume

Chapter 1

Inspector Clements

"Strangled?" Inspector Clements enquired.

"It appears that way, sir," replied PC Palmer. Clements took a closer look at the body slumped upon the chair. He noted there was reddening around the throat.

"It does look that way, least at first glance. There are finger marks present though I suspect they were not the ones doing the killing. See the impression of nails dug in at the top here? These, I believe, were those of the victim fighting to remove whatever it was around his throat. Check for traces of skin under the fingernails. The red banding suggests a belt or rope of some description, a large one at that. He must have been taken by surprise; either that or his attacker possessed great strength, more likely both."

"Yes, that makes sense. Queer thing is, no one saw or heard a thing. Not even the dogs were roused. No sign of a struggle either."

"I see. That is most extraordinary given the racket those animals made when I came in."

"No sign of a break-in either, sir; nothing stolen or damaged in anyway," Palmer replied, in askance.

"Except this poor man."

"Yes, sir."

"How do we know it was not one of the staff?"

"There is a domestic who lives here; tiny little thing. She didn't hear anything at all. It was her who found the body. Looks a harmless sort to me, sir. She is downstairs, in a terrible state. The gamekeeper's wife is with her."

"Some of the deadliest killers of all look harmless enough, Palmer, forget you not."

"Yes. No sir, I will not."

"Good."

"There was one thing though. It is probably nothing really. The domestic believes she saw a snake in the house earlier in the evening. A large one at that. She told Mr Faber about it. They searched everywhere but found nothing."

"Could have been a Python I suppose. But what on earth would it being doing here?
Where is the man's wife?"

"She is at her sister's in Paris. We have not been able to contact her yet."

"Then how do you know she is in Paris?"

"I... I don't, sir, least that is where she is supposed to be."

"Very well. Come, let's go and speak to this domestic then."

"You don't think this could be the work of that escaped prisoner, Jemmet do you sir?"

"Impossible to say at present. He is certainly a fellow that holds grudges."

Chapter 2

Botanical Wonders

"To understand another creature or botanical wonder, one has to immerse oneself in its very soul, swim the rivers of its being, explore the luxuriant density of its scent, its swollen self. Pay special regard to its natural surroundings, interactions, and motivations," Adam Cuttlebrook enthused to Mr Hufflewaite of Her Royal Majesty's Botanical Institute.

"I see that you not only have a flair for the production of plants but a deep passion for them."

"Indeed I do, sir, but not just plants, insects too. If it were not for insects, there would be no plants and therefore no *us*. One cannot exist without the cooperation of the... other," Adam replied, with earnest exuberance to begin with but as his reply drew to a close it became laboured, reflective. He pointed to his voluminous glasshouse inside where bees drifted in and out of the blooms, covered in pollen.

"Quite so, but as you very well know, these *others* you refer to can also be their downfall too, can they not?"

"Why, of course. Just imagine how magical it would be if we could interact with these strange beings, though. Maybe then we could gain insights into their drives and appetites. Just imagine how useful that could be? Through our understanding, we could compose devise a way to control them, as opposed to poisoning them. Call it more a distraction or misdirection. But first we need to communicate with them."

Hufflewaite regarded Cuttlebrook warily, unsure as to whether he should be in awe or disturbed by the other man's fantastical aspirations. *Are you a madman or a genius?* was the unsaid question upon his lips. He deliberated on such an utterance but decided it that it would have been impudent of him to do so. Especially as Cuttlebrook was presently confounding the botanical world with new varieties of plants with outstanding vigour, unparalleled length of bloom and floral longevity.

Cuttlebrook was not oblivious to the fact that Hufflewaite's expression of curiosity had been superseded by one of pensive apprehension. He was used to such a look when waxing lyrical about his ideas to men such as Hufflewaite. It frustrated him and he grew tired of seeking a similar vision amongst his contemporaries. *I suppose I should make one last effort*, Adam decided, groaning inwardly.
"Do not misunderstand me, sir. It would be impossible for us to have anything other than a small foothold in their huge kingdom. Plants and insects are

too powerful for us to have anything more than that. Indeed, one could argue that we are little more than puppets to them."

"I am afraid you have lost me there, Cuttlebrook. What do you mean?" Hufflewaite declared, scrunching his eyes, as if this small act would help him gain purchase of Cuttlebrook's rationale.

"It is fundamental, really. Look at plants for instance. Do we not willingly produce more of them every day? We spread their seed far and wide across the globe, further than any wind could blow or bird could carry them."

"Point taken. However, we are the engineers of such an industry, are we not? And do not forget, we harvest a great many of them for food, medicine and other utilities. Surely that makes us the masters of them, not vice versa?"

"Maybe they would like us to think that way," Cuttlebrook retorted mischievously, before continuing, "but we need them far more than they need us. Perhaps we are but a means to an end for them. Of course, we can destroy great swathes of vegetation in a thrice, but if we were to stand back and see the world as a whole, it is they and their insect collaborators who have the upper hand."

"I can understand what you are getting at, but what if, sometime in the future, we kill them all by accident, poison them? Surely that makes us the masters of their fate?"

"I would not put it past us, though we would not be masters, would we? Fools more like. Masters of our own demise, I suppose, as death would follow swiftly should we be so foolhardy. I would still wager that plants and insects would out live us all in one shape or form."

"Yes, perhaps so, but you will still have to forgive me. I cannot endorse the idea that we are little more than pawns to them. If I was a religious man, Cuttlebrook, I would suspect there is something heretical in your supposition. Be thankful that I am not," replied Hufflewaite with a wry smile.

Cuttlebrook grinned, nodding his head as he often did when faced with incredulity.

"You obviously do not hear their voices as I do, sir." Almost as soon as the words had left his lips, Cuttlebrook regretted their utterance. Hufflewaite surmised that he either had spent too long by himself, or in the company of his beloved *others*.

Chapter 3

Ragwort

It had been just over three years since Adam had moved back to Shabbington House. His father Sidney had left him the estate in his will. Not that his father had had much trust in Adam's ability to manage it correctly. He had still seen the thirty year old man as a dreamy child. Adam's elder sister had already had her share of the family's money whilst their father was still alive. Most of it had been ploughed into the jet mine she ran with her husband on the Yorkshire coast. Adam's great aunt Lu, of whom he was very fond, had died only two weeks before her brother Sidney, giving Adam sole control over house and grounds. Before taking over the estate, Adam had thrown himself into the study of horticulture. His plan was to repair and extend the greenhouses already present upon the estate. Their great aunt had been a keen amateur horticulturalist and had carried on the tradition of growing plants which had begun with his grandparents.

As luck would have it, Tom, the estate's ageing gardener, was keen to assist in his plans. Tom had worked for the family for over fifty years and had known Adam's great grandparents as a lad. The gardener taught the new master of the house everything he could not find out from a text book. Adam considered him to be part and parcel of the estate just as the place where he now headed; the St Ethwold's Church.

The spot of past reverence lay across a fallow field and in amongst a stand of weeds and yellowing grasses. The church was situated on the outskirts of his family's estate. His father once said that a church had stood in this same position since Saxon times. Its doors had been shut for over twenty years, and signs of neglect were visible to all. Adam was reluctant to condemn or mend the venerable place. Nowadays it was little more than a folly, a relic, a place to romanticise about the past. Adam had shed his skin and lost faith in a traditional form of worship many years since. He had found a greater meaning within the realms of sea, sky and earth.

Despite this loss of faith, he could not free himself of the sentiment he still felt towards it. Whether it was due to the reverence given to it by his family, or a monumental reminder of blood line's long association with it and its surrounds, he did not know. His father's family had been baptised, married and buried here for hundreds of years. Once he reached his parents' graveside, he placed some dried blue statice and cornflowers upon it. The grave along with that of his great aunt Lu's and his grandparents, was at least well-tended. Tom's grandson Luke saw to this with a scythe. The rest of the churchyard was left to a greater power.

Whenever he walked here, he was never without kin; inseparable from those that had been before him. Their weight of expectation upon him often caused him to stride swiftly through the yard. It was a bid to deny their very existence. Today, though, was not one of those days. He knelt to observe the caterpillars of Cinnabar moths gorging upon a ragwort.

"How beautiful you are, my dears, and how poisonous!" Adam exclaimed, aware that this particular insect was one of the few creatures that could eat this plant without serious retribution. It was a source of nutrition as well as protection for it, too. Far from killing the adult moth or its preceding caterpillars, it protected its consumer from predators, thus rendering it repellent at best, deadly at worst, to its prey. *Perhaps we are all surrounded with a little poison,* he mused.

Chapter 4

Toad

"Your tea will not be long. Toad in the hole, your favourite,' said Molly, pointing at the stove.

"Great, about time we had some of that. Did you put rosemary in the batter?" Tom asked, removing his coat.

"Yes, as always. You had a good day?"

"Aye, not bad. Bloody icy blast out there, though. Thankfully, I have been in the greenhouses for most of it. At least the boiler is working properly now. I keep telling Adam that I ain't a plumber, but he always insists we try and sort it out ourselves."

"Perhaps he is a bit short of money. You never can tell with them folk?"

"Nah, reckon not. He is no businessman, but there is plenty of interest in the plants he is producing. Buggers are flying out of the door."

"I am sure it is as much down to you as it is to him."

"No, Molly, it ain't. I have taught him a lot, that is true, but there is a lot more to it than that. You should see the growth on 'em."

"Maybe he has just got green fingers. You always said Lu did. Maybe he takes after her."

"She did, that is true, but this isn't just an affinity, this is...I don't know really. It is almost like he is a charmer, you know, like how you say your brother can charm away warts, Adam charms plants. I have no other word for it. It doesn't seem natural, not that it bothers me. Some things are outside of our understanding, I s'pose -certainly above mine."

"God works in mysterious ways, doesn't he? Charm plants though! Indeed! Ha ha! Well, I do declare, Thomas Burfitt, it isn't at all like you to give ideas such as that the time of day."

"No, it isn't. Believe me, I have no other explanation; unless he has got secret formulas tucked away, and doses 'em up when I'm not there."

"More than likely, daft old sod that you are."

"You haven't been up there for a while. Come up with me soon, then you will see. Never mind that for now. Give me a hand getting these boots off, woman. You will be on to me for dirtying your rug if I don't," replied Thomas, laughing.

Chapter 5

Transformation - Diary extract

Since returning to this house my empathy towards the natural world feels stronger than ever. For the most part I believe this is a good and noble disposition, though I am not without concern. I believe I possess a far stronger affinity with plants, insects and other such creatures than anyone I have ever come across. That said, I cannot confess that I was always keen to embrace the broad horizon of what this understanding offered. There were times when I found it disturbing. This exaggerated sense of awareness was not only a mystery to me but others too.

In my latter years at school I did my best to evade the clutches of the natural world. It was as though it intruded upon my being. I was laughed at when I mentioned that I could feel the bristling of fern or hear the distant hatching of a bird. I feared I was strange; unnatural. It was not so much as a burden, more of unbidden distraction, especially where my schooling was concerned. I was quick to realise other people did not possess this intimacy. If they did, they must have been able to subjugate such an awareness. I believe all children feel a sense of wonderment at, and in, the natural world to begin with; though this is often lost in adulthood. However, there is a difference between wonderment and complete immersion which is what I felt. Because I could not achieve that sense of detachedness I rarely, if ever, discussed the matter. I wish to state for the record, though, that I was not always so acutely aware of the movements and moments of the natural world. I shall enlarge upon this later.

My "difference" as a child was put down to having a fertile imagination; a dweller in cloud-cuckoo-land. These were the kindest description references to my detachment. There was some truth in the cuckoo-land part, at least. I always had the distinct impression that I was a cuckoo in the nest; not an unwanted one, but out of place.

I am sure this difference in my state of awareness came upon me around the age of seven. I suspect it was born out of, or triggered, by a solitary incident. It occurred during the time I lived in Ceylon with my family. I had spent most of my childhood there, and regarded it, as opposed to Shabbington House, as my home. Despite being born in the village of Shabbington, and visiting its willowy waters regularly, most of my youth was spent in that far off wild, steamy and floriferous place.

My father had had a prominent position at the British Embassy in Ceylon. Fortunately, he rarely talked about his role there, as, when he did, I found it dreadfully dull. My mother was frequently homesick and often read out letters to my elder sister Ann and I. Most of the correspondence came from Great Aunt Lu who ran the Shabbington estate, though there were other letters, usually from cousins and such.

As a child, the thing I enjoyed the most was exploration. It was a pastime from which I was neither discouraged or encouraged. The fact that I was allowed to escape quite so freely is something I find truly remarkable now. My parents were sticklers for manners and etiquette, yet there was I roaming around a largely untamed jungle. Of course, there were rules about such forays; never go on my own, never to stay out for longer than three hours, and never to go out if heavy rain was expected. I am pleased to say, though, that most of these rules I regularly ignored without much ado.

It was upon such an escapade that everything in my life altered. The day was like most others, smothered in golden sunshine. Sometime between breakfast and midday, Charlie and I wandered through the village and into the jungle. He was three years older than I and was the son of my mother's maid. Some way into

our adventure Charlie wandered off to a local basin where the local fishermen often gathered. He assured me that he would not be long, but I grew impatient and decided to go off on my own. I had little or no fear at that age.

My elder companion was often my chaperone and guide on these random sojourns. We rarely, if ever, ventured far from the established paths, but in his absence, I was determined to see as much of the, as yet, previously unexplored places as I possibly could. Quite how far I meandered I do not know; time had little meaning to me then, whereas the yearning to investigate new territory held much. Every virgin step brought new sights and sounds erstwhile unbeknown to me. I was fascinated by the abundance of the carnivorous plant known to me as the "pitcher plant." I had only seen this before in a painting but had heard tell it was called *Bandura* by the natives. It creeps up and through all of the other foliage.

My sister had told me how this peculiar specimen eats insects for it to grow. I could not resist peering into its red lips and speckled, hollow mouth. The bottom of its jug shaped throat was where it digested its prey. Sure enough, its base was sticky and there were a number of forlorn insects inside. Each had suffered the ill fortune to have fallen into its lair.

Although curious, I never plucked up the courage to actually stick my finger into such a weird thing.

As my eye wandered over its leaves, I saw, nearby, a most dazzling butterfly. It was unlike anything I had ever laid eyes on beforehand. I wanted to take a closer look, so I strode over to where it was perched. My youthful clumsiness must have startled it for as I drew close it flew off; zigzagging this way and that. Such was the brilliance of its multi-hued wings against the emerald green of the jungle, I never lost sight of it. So determined was I to get a better view, I swear I scarcely blinked in my pursuit of the creature. Its erratic flight seemed to follow an old winding path.

My feet became sodden due to the damp foliage under foot, though this deterred me not. I tracked this be-winged beauty for quite a distance before it stopped upon a bloom. I moved ever nearer to it, with what I believed was much stealth, taking care not to get snagged on a vine or protruding root, of which there were many. On closer inspection, the butterfly was more exquisite than I dared to have dreamt. It had turquoise and amber stripes on its wings, interspersed with golden circles filled with violet. These exquisite markings made it appear like a pair of eyes fluttering upon the breeze. I cupped my hands as I moved closer. I did not want to hurt it, just hold it, even for a second. To my mind I believed it more precious than gold. I wanted to feel it walk upon my skin, embrace its delicacy, its elusiveness. A branch snapped beneath me, my balance faltered, my cherished quarry took flight once more.

When I got back upon my feet the creature danced before me, as if it were teasing me. I dared not attempt to clasp my hands around it when in flight; that would have meant a cruel end for such beauty. After about twenty paces, it came to rest upon a mossy stump amongst a tangle of vines and ferns. This, I believed, was where I would catch it. I pictured myself as a leopard as I ran towards it, imagining myself to have terrific speed. It would be mine. I saw nothing other than my prey, but just as I was about to touch it, the ground gave way beneath me. What I presumed was a part of the jungle floor evidently was not. I recall rolling downwards for what felt like an eternity, before bashing my head. After that there was nothingness, a void that lasted for how long, I do not know.

My limbs felt so stiff I was unable to move. It did not feel like the stiffness of fatigue; no, this was more akin to being bound to invisible sticks. Judging by the layer of debris I had to blow off my face, I must have been lying there quite a while. My body was also clothed in twigs, insects and spent leaves. It was as if the jungle had swallowed me up, taken me inside itself. At the time I was not unduly alarmed by this, least not as much as by the pain in my head. I felt the urge to stand but it was beyond me, such was the rigidity of my limbs. My skin was moist but not what I would describe as cold.

After that first flicker of consciousness, my self-awareness came and went (along with the rain). I can vaguely recall being aware of the slow onset of night and the relief of the dawn. The tantalizingly slow drift between light and dark has left an indelible imprint upon my memory. My first recollection of experiencing an unadulterated dawn was one of total rapture…a light that did not fade, one that got brighter and brighter. And the birdsong…it was like being caught in a shower of rain in a wide, open meadow; first you feel a single droplet, then another, then many until saturated. That was how the avians serenaded the dawn. They stung my ears with joy. Since that day I have taken the liberty to suppose that there would be no dawn without a bird present to guide its celestial passage.

It took some time before I had the vaguest notion as to what and who I was, where I lived, and with whom. After many failed attempts at standing up, I succeeded. Once upright, I brushed myself free of all of the insects and cocoons which had erstwhile made me their home. I found sunlight, though dappled, too much to bear, so I sought shade. I must have looked like a stumbling infant to any onlookers, of which there were none. Though I say *none* I do not believe that to have been wholly true. I had the distinct notion that there was another human presence close by, not one that I could see or hear, but one was, I am sure. From that day to this, I have not felt truly alone, which I believe was a consequence of that fall, or that place, or something I know not what.

When I reassured myself that I could stand, I took a brief respite upon a log. Once seated, I tried to take stock of what had happened to me and muster up some kind of plan. This was an arduous task as I was becoming more aware of pain. My body was covered in small cuts and big, black bruises. One of my ankles was sprained; as for my head…that ached to high heaven. That injury was the cause of the scar upon my forehead, which is still all too apparent today. I placed my hand upon it, and quickly removed it again. There was dried blood upon my fingers. In hindsight it was a miracle no infection had set in.

Through shaded eyes I surveyed the landscape around me. I was in the bottom of a large hollow, not unreminiscent of an old quarry, surrounded by a girdle of ferns, vines and trees. Insects scurried about and flew all around me, especially in the area in which I had since lain. I could hear their movements, almost, and understood their endeavours. They, like every other living thing, were no longer *just* themselves: insects, ferns, trees, or vines. They were vastly more…real. Each very much *alive,* teaming with what I can only describe as an electric vivacity unique unto itself. Even sedentary beings such as trees murmured and twitched, pulsed even. The ferns emanated a gentle hiss, not unlike that of a snake. They also seemed to possess an aura, though not a definitive band of light; more an indistinct ring of moisture that sparkled in the sunlight. As for the vines, they bristled and ticked.

Other things came back to me slowly over time. Whether this malady was a symptom of the injury to my head l know not. It was as if I had lost part of my old self and found a new one. I had acquired a fresh sense of perception and of place in the world around me. I suspect many would have been quite disturbed by this newfound sensitivity but I was not, at least not immediately or overwhelmingly so.

Of course, it would have been impossible to have felt alone with all this life encircling me; but there was an overriding sense of another human present which perturbed me the most. Despite scanning every horizon for evidence of this *other,* I saw no one. Although I was concerned, nothing could remove my new-found sense of awe that I felt in the jungle - not only in its sum, but its many parts too. It was a conscious being, free from the bondage of morality and pretence. Of course, I could only define these observations upon reaching adulthood, though I believe I felt them at the time as well. Contrary to much of modern thinking, I do not believe this lack of conscience is wholly detrimental or a base thing. After all is it not the chief instinct of all things to *exist and survive,* regardless of method or the metre of its verse?

I pushed myself up with much determination and made my way towards the generous shade offered by a gigantic tree. To my surprise, under its muscular boughs lay a partially sunken ruin. Almost buried under a blanket of detritus and moss, the building was only just discernible. The thought of exploring it exhilarated me. My arboreal companion's serpentine roots penetrated deep into its cavities. It was now my time to do likewise. Despite the pain, my curiosity propelled me through the vines and over tree roots which ran down the hollow like wax from a candle.

So bleak was its inside, it felt as though I had walked into a featureless tomb, until two broken rays of light bored through its dilapidated roof enabling me to see markings upon the walls. I had imagined the air inside to have been sour, heavy with damp abandonment, but it was not. Truthfully though, if there were any residues of such malodorous and melancholic odours, they were well masked. The only smell I was aware of was the scent of musk, a sweet one, too. Not unlike that of a Parisian whore at sunset, but that is another story. So rich was this ancient place's perfume I (latterly) doubted it could have been a temple at all...However, I digress. Given the reliefs on the walls, I do think it must have been a place of worship, but of what, I know not.

The deep lines etched up the stones seemed, with hindsight, to represent a creation tale. People with wings, emanating from a fracture in the earth. Plants and creatures were just as flamboyant, many displaying human characteristics too. Not all of the images I witnessed on that day were as inspiring, though. Upon another wall, sparse of light, lay ominous images; scenes of murder and destruction abounded. Needless to say, my eyes did not linger upon such frightful depictions. As much as I wished to further explore this cavernous feast, I was overcome by an immediate need to eat, to drink. God knows how long it was since I had eaten or drunk anything at all.

After dragging myself through the thick undergrowth of the hollow, I set about re-tracing my steps back home. Despite my sorry state, I located the path that had taken me there. The deeply etched footway was no more than a strand now, barely traceable amongst the foliage. Upon reflection, my chances of finding that trail home had been almost non-existent. Was this instinctual? Maybe...

It was nightfall when I returned to the place that I vaguely recalled as being my home. My parents were utterly aghast to see me. I was puzzled by the look of fear in my mother's eyes. Maybe that observation was ill founded, brought on by over-worked imagination. I cannot say, but from that day onwards I always detected a sense of suspicion from those close to me. Perhaps it was because they did not believe my account of what had happened. I doubt I shall ever know. I recall being questioned endlessly about it. Ann believed me, or at least she said she did. She told me that my parents had given up all hope of finding me alive. Search parties had been sent out in every direction imaginable. Charlie had evidently been chastised severely for letting me wander off. Despite my insistence to the contrary, he still took most of the blame for the affair. No wonder he did not want anything to do with me afterwards.

Chapter 6

Mr and Mrs Nicholls

"When are you going to snuff out that candle, Maria?"

"I'm still reading,"

"No, you aren't. You keep holding the book up to your face then moving it to one side. You have been agitated for hours now, have you not?"

"No... well, yes, I have,"

"What is the matter?"

"I told you, there is something or someone in the house with us."

"Oh that..." Stuart Nicholls said dismissively, losing interest.

"See, you don't want to know the answer. Why bother asking if you don't want to know the answer?"

"The house creaks, all houses creak, especially the old ones. We've only been here a few weeks. You are just not used to the noises yet. It is part of the personality of the house."

"It has nothing to do with the creaks. I told you earlier the curtain moved, as if something brushed up against it."

Mr Nicholls sighed and said,

"It is the wind then. That room faces north and there is a hellish north wind tonight."

"This wasn't the wind. Something brushed against it."

"I will sort that out in the morning, that's after we plant out those huge lavender bushes you insisted on buying up the road."

"It wasn't only that. Something moved upon the rug, too,"

"Mice!" Mr Nicholls responded.

"This was no mouse." Mrs Nicholls whispered her reply,

"It is the shadow of the flames from the fire then. As I said to you earlier, it is an unusually strong blast tonight."

"There is something here now, listen." Mr Nicholls sat up. They both held their breath.

The silence accentuated the yap of a neighbour's dog from a few doors down. Mr Nicholls fumbled around for his matches and lit his candle. A small speck of lighted match spat across the room when he struck the match against the box. He cursed and leapt out of the bed; stubbing out the glowing speck with his bare feet. The candle he had lit dragged a long shadow across the room. He turned and glowered at Mrs Nicholls.

Mrs Nicholls was too consumed with anxiety to take heed to her husband's unspoken rebuke. Mr Nicholls shielded the flame protectively and made towards the bedroom door. Once at the door, he looked back towards his wife before turning the handle. Cold air poured in. Mrs Nicholls rubbed her arms vigorously. This was not only a reaction to the drop-in temperature; it was to soothe her frayed nerves as well.

"If it means we will both get some sleep, I will have a look around the house!" bellowed Mr Nicholls. His wife nodded, though did not reply. It was not that she did not wish to; fear refused to grant her voice wings. So, there they remained, perched inside the back of her throat.

Mr Nicholls shut the door onto the landing. Mrs Nicholls heard a low mumble from outside of the room. The sound, she presumed, emanated from her irate husband muttering and sighing at the inconvenience of it all. The flame upon her beside candle was slow to settle after the door was closed upon her. Once the flame was at peace, Mrs Nicholls' eye was caught by the webbing in the far corner of the room. She had not yet found time to attend to all of the chores the new house demanded.

A tapestry of spiders' silks hung upon the wall, thick with dust and littered with indistinct specks of black. The lifeless husks caused her to shudder. She could not rest until they were removed, though she was too afeared to move. When her husband returned, she would get him to tear them down. She was both repulsed and arrested by the arachnids' hoary labours.

Something is moving within the webs. Look, it is twitching. Mrs Nicholls watched on in horror. Screwing up her eyes to focus she detected movement within the web. Although no culprit was to be seen the silken threads twitched. *It has seen me looking upon it, it waits for me,* Mrs Nicholls thought whilst pulling up the eiderdown. In the distance she heard her husband slam the shed door. *It has been swollen by the heavy showers. Yet another thing to attend to,* she sighed inwardly. The fire crackled and spat out an ember onto the fireguard. It was dying now. The noise averted her gaze away from the lair of the unseen spider back towards the closed bedroom door. The pale light from the lamp upon the landing silhouetted the edges of the door, highlighting the large gap at the top. At least it had until now.

The usual, distinctive glow was no more. It had become smudged, disordered. Accompanying this transformation was an almost inaudible hum. The distorted band of light had become absorbed by diminutive shadows, multiplying by the second. These parcels of shade began to spread from their pale slice of light around the room. The tiny specs congealed like oil upon a watery canvas. Individuals they still were, but they had gathered into something stronger, rising and falling like waves upon the tired wallpaper.

Where has that damn man gone to? Mrs Nicholls ruminated fretfully as the smudges swam across the room to the wall where the head of the bed stood. She sank into the cold linen as their hum transformed to a hateful buzz. The collective shadows intensified to a swarm upon the headboard. The fear-torn lady froze as they conspired behind her. Something brushed against her unbound hair, but she remained quite still. Her eyes shot to her right, hoping the congealment would accompany them.

The fringe of the malignant shadow duly obliged but the heart of the swarm stayed behind her. So loud was the sound emanating from this dreadful anomaly, she wanted to raise her hands to her ears - but she dared not move. There was a footfall upon the bottom step. Her eyes widened. These were no longer just shadows upon the insentient, cool and flat lines of the wall. She felt a tickle upon her left ear, then her temple. The space between her hair and the back of her neck became congested. Her hands set as in aspic. A bonnet of insects adorned Mrs Nicholls' head, unleashing an abomination of needles. Her scream pierced and tattooed on the mind of Mr Nicholls forever. Her piercing scream was tattooed on the mind of Mr Nicholls forever.

31

The bed bubbled up in a monstrous mass of movement. Mr Nicholls saw a dark cloud fly over his head when he entered the room. He instinctively raised his hands to protect his face. It passed out and onto the landing. He slammed the door shut, at a loss as to what he had seen. Rushing over to the bed, he gazed down at a mound of crumpled sheets and the twitching remains of Mrs Nicholls. Stung beyond recognition.

Chapter 7

Application - Diary extract

I am now in no doubt whatsoever that my empathy with my botanical specimens is having significant results upon the yield and vigour of my stock. As much as I would almost like to prove myself wrong, I am at a loss for any other explanation. I have no greater resources than any other grower or nurseryman (except of course Tom, who is invaluable). We do not possess any superior food or compost; no advanced heating systems or greenhouses more capable that the others. The seeds I use are from the same suppliers that others use.

I am somewhat hesitant to record my methods, if one could ever call such immersion a method in the first place. I once tried to explain my ideas to another and was mocked mercilessly so there will be no more of that. I have no inkling whether or not this route would work for someone else. It produces results for me, so I care not. The fact that it *does* work is the primary reason I wish to record such incidences.

The instance I had when experimenting with the production of citron trees is a fine example. First, I cleared my head of all other clutter and focussed upon the plants in the eye of my mind. I travelled back with them to the foothills of their place of origin, in this case it was the Himalayas. First you feel their pulse, experience the sun upon their skin, sense the power of the sun upon the leaf. Once engaged with their entirety you have the power, as it were, to liberate them.

I know exactly when I have reached the point of true empathy. It is utter exhilaration; running through one's senses like rapids in a crevasse. An unparalleled feeling of both intoxication and lucidity, power and powerlessness. The totality of the flood upon one's being is complete. It is as though you have entered into its cells, its very soul.

Of course, such a submersion and its subsequent effects upon the specimens would be impossible to corroborate scientifically, but that is of little or no concern to me. I can see the effects with my own eyes; the diverse and wondrous ways which such communication yields. In most incidences size, vigour and fragrance dramatically increase. This, matched with a higher resistance to both pest and disease, astonishes me. Every so often, I do incur mutations. These sad specimens either fail miserably or go off into strange and unwanted directions. The bulk of the latter group I keep in a glasshouse separate from the rest, a precaution against cross pollination. Thankfully though, these cases are few and far between. On the whole, I have been overwhelmed by the progress we have made.

The only fly-in-the-ointment, as it were, is that I have an inkling that the effects of this deep botanical communion may not be so beneficial for me. I have come to the conclusion that something extraordinary occurred when I had my first (albeit totally instinctive) deep empathy with a botanical specimen here in Shabbington. I doubt it has any link to the temporary loss of mental control one goes through whence engaged in these experiments, though I would not rule out it unbalancing another.

Mercifully, I have not suffered any declension of character, or force of will. Although I cannot say for definite, I think it could well be assisting this *other* closer to me. The awareness of, or presence of what I have termed the *other,* seems greatly increased. It is the same presence that I have been aware of since my accident in the hollow. To liken it to the feeling of being watched would be an understatement. As a sensation it is impossible to convey with any sense of clarity or definition, even less with any credibility. I just know it to be there. I feel it. Sounds that should not occur, occur. Things fall to the ground that should not fall. I am forever searching for it, trying to catch it out of the corner of my eye yet never see it. It is cunning.

When it is near, I sense resentment; a troubled spirit perhaps? It exudes upon me a melancholy and meanness which I do not consider to be inherent traits of mine. Even when I am dreaming it shares images of evil intent. At least I hope it be only intent. When I awaken from these nocturnal visitations my bones are like Arctic snow, frigid and raw. I even suspected that I may have a baleful twin that was lost to me, taken away before I knew it. One that I could pick up on its thoughts; some strange, brooding, other half.

I learnt to live with it around me because I had to, and it seemed of little encumbrance then. Alas, the same cannot be said now. No longer is it a twitching chrysalis rustling in the undergrowth of my senses. Is it possible for a person to haunt himself?

I am all too aware that the act of writing these words crystallizes its shadow upon me. I just feel I ought to, so others may later know what afflicts me so. There could, of course, be another option as to why I feel the way I do (though not one I wish to adhere to or give any credence to at present). Namely, that it is a consequence of being encircled with doubt after the occurrence at the hollow. My waking up in an alien environment, swarming with others, seen and unseen, leached up my reasoning in some way, corrupting my nervous system.

Alas, I have digressed. I have veered by leap and by bound away from my initial purpose of this entry, that being to note the remarkable effects of my communion upon my green flock. I do not know from where this gift derives, because it is, despite all else, a wondrous gift. I recognize that I have in my possession a tool of sublime potency and wonder.

Chapter 8

Dear Brother - A letter from Ann

It is with great interest that I read about the success you and Tom are having at the old place. Do tell me that your innovations are matched with a modicum of financial gain. I know you. You are a dreamer if ever there was one and would not realize your own poverty until the shirt fell off your back. As I have not heard to the contrary, I take it you have not yet found yourself a suitor? You really should have stayed with Susannah you know; she was a good sort, probably too good for you. Do get your skates on though, Adam. Regretfully, it seems I may pass through life without issue, so I am relying on you to sow the seed.

I hope you are keeping the house in good repair. I will be checking you know. It is no good rolling your eyes; believe me you must keep on top of these things or else they will go to rack and ruin within a blink of an eye. Matthew and I plan to visit when we get a spare weekend. Have no fear though, we will give you plenty of advance notice before hand. I hope the new housekeeper is settling in well. Such a shame that Dorothy left, she was a good old stick. Do not ignore her. A little company will do you the world of good.

Oh, and do not forget, your sister knows what is good for you.

Best wishes,
Ann X

Chapter 9

Carnivorous - Diary extract

I have spent the entire day in the hot house. The boiler uses a lot of coal, but it is vital the temperatures are kept up. This hot house excites me no end. Tom and I have finally fixed the irrigation system. We can mist all the plants at once when needs be. Our species count goes up weekly. One would expect a small set-back to the plants' progress when a plant is moved from one environment to another, though as yet this has not happened.

I am especially pleased that our carnivorous specimens are thriving. I have an entire greenhouse devoted to Nepenthes distillatoria, most commonly called the "pitcher plant." I have not lost any of my initial intrigue in these insectivorous delights of Ceylon. Their culture, form and function absorb me. The way they gain their strength through slowly devouring their prey; sitting patiently, waiting for their quarry to fall into their gaping mouths. Strange to say, there is something peculiarly gratifying in producing such plants as these. As perverse as it sounds, I quite like the idea of plants feeding upon insects rather than the other way around; a form of equilibrium.

My aim, other than producing these botanical wonders, is to use them as a form of pest control. If we could devise some large enough and adaptable enough to use in most greenhouses, we could cut down our use of insecticide significantly. And not just in *our* houses, but throughout the land. First, we need to formulate a way to lower the temperatures in which they can survive. This will take some time, but I believe it is achievable. Everything at the moment seems achievable.

Chapter 10

Bromeliads - Diary extract

My dreams have become much more vivid of late, none more so than the one that stole upon me yesterday afternoon. Not that I am given to sleeping during the afternoon unless I have partaken of too much port, of course. The seeds of my unintentional journey into dreamland arose after I fell a-slumber in a glasshouse dedicated to plants of the tropics. Tom and I had been engaged in propagation of air plants, specifically bromeliads. Just for the record, these intriguing beings (sometimes called urn plants, due to their ability to store water in an urn shaped union at the foot of the plant) grow upon the branches of trees in the Brazilian rainforests. They need little to no roots as their leaves give them all of the food necessary.

After completing the task, I sent Tom off to make a start on pruning the orchard, leaving me to tidy up. I began to reflect on what we had just done and the marvel of air plants. After a short while I became sleepy and a little dizzy; detached from my surroundings. I brushed the soil off my hands and sat upon a wooden box and leant back against the wall. I was grateful it was there, otherwise I think I would have collapsed in a heap upon the floor.

I doubt that this *separation* was born out of my labour alone. Perhaps it had sprung from my absorption of bromeliads themselves upon my skin? I would like to think it was that that had triggered such a flight of fancy, but I cannot be sure. There was something subtly different about this instance, the depth of its allure that left me somewhat undone by its intrusion and splendour afterwards.

I feel the need to record details of this journey unbidden, once clear in my mind, if only to clear a course back to the present, such was the intoxication of the flight. This account is not wholly linear, I know dreams (if that is what it was) rarely are; though this was no ordinary sojourn into the world of the sleeper. My first remembrance of this flight was a vision of a butterfly, not unlike the one I had seen in the hollow. The soft and silent beat of its wings became one with the beat of my heart, opening it fully to the misty world of the bromeliads.

I needed not to touch my brow to know it was beaded with sweat; my skin was adorned by a cloak of liquid pearls. The roar of the forest immediately beseeched my serenity, as an explosion of noise. So disparate and numerous were its emissions; it became a veritable orchestra of sound. I must confess that its initial foray upon my senses was somewhat alarming, though within less than a minute I was swept asunder by its rhapsody; wondrous yet terrible in its enormity.

The strings shimmered through the air; distant violins of water falling. Every leaf that fell, cascaded like harp-song upon the ear. Horns and woodwinds pierced through verdant corridors of the forest; bird and beak, soft, sharp and shrill. Under a lavender sky the pulse-like drumming from inside the trees thumped out, deep and sombre as the grave. There was an incalculable sum of other noises as well; too numerous and diverse to describe or compare. These utterances, I believe, stemmed from insects carpeting the forest floor, others on the wing or perched, as was I, watching. Oh, and frogs. How could I ever forget their almost unearthly croak, though if the truth must be told, I almost wanted to.

The paucity of light was dissected by hungry tongues of green - fronds and blades alike. The sun was no more than a smudge of mustard, a misty martyr, diffused and shallow in sermon. The very ground I looked upon moved like a river; ants carried debris high above their heads, muttering. It was as though they were involved in some kind of religious parade

or ritual, holding votive offerings and icons upon high, saluting the gods of the forest.

Water droplets fell to earth whilst others embellished and baptised an abundance of webs. Their moistened silk threads resembled bridal veils as the sun fastened its gaze upon their shimmering fibres. Each possessed a weave unique to itself, intricate, though purposeful, strong yet submissive; delicate and melodious upon the eye.

As my senses trickled through the silvery gauze, I became liberated from the eggshell. All things became much more terrible and far more beautiful at once. A dragonfly emerging, wings a-glisten, from years of safe harbour below a dense and watery film. I beheld the texture of the world as would a blind man. I heard, smelt and swam in the voracious whirlpool of the senses. The warm embrace of a feather and its soft wind of flight upon my face. The heat of a big cat's breath, the movement of the fangs, the thick sticky liquid that lies across its tongue…. I tasted all.

This was much more lucid than any dream. A dream implies an imagined state, and this was anything but. The things I saw were real, not flickering images, or unrelated fears or scenes. So genuine was its expression that I felt my entire being had been transported away by an unseen hand and placed upon the branch of a tree. After all, there were no witnesses to the contrary and when I eventually awakened, I was saturated in sweat and the scent of moss and the unrecognised tree upon which I dwelt.

My slumber was brought to an end by a terrifying growl of an unseen (but not unfelt) beast out of my vision. For a while my reality was spliced between the two worlds. Bewildered, I stumbled to my propagation bench. I looked upon the rows of bromeliads. They were no longer *just* offsets of urn plants now. They were vast vaults of memory and sensory experience, a world within a world. I eventually forced myself into a detachment from them; no easy task.

Post script - four weeks later - Diary extract

Every one of the offsets of bromeliads I potted up that day have survived and taken with frightful ease; some even show signs of flowering which, under normal circumstances, would be preposterous - though I now realize that I am no longer working in the lair of normal circumstances.

Chapter 11

Recollections - Diary extract

The sense of this *other* appears ever more prevalent.
Whether this presence springs forth from hitherto
unexplored recesses of my mind, I cannot be sure. I
would pull it out by the roots if I could yet but find it.
At worst, compartmentalize it and place it into the
understood compartment in my head. As I recorded
earlier, this uninvited guest first drew breath after the
incident in the jungle. So, with this in mind I decided
to review my recollections of what happened directly
after it.

Not long after I had returned home, we were visited
by our family's physician Doctor Tewson (and the all-
pervading scent of cinnamon which accompanied him
everywhere). I am led to believe he came specifically
to examine me. He greeted me with a smile, albeit a
slightly hesitant and insipid one. I remember his
crumpled white suit, white beard and unkempt hair
(what was left of it anyway). At the time I likened his
face to that of a weasel. His skin looked like burnt
orange peel, befitting a man of half British and half
Indian extraction that had been out in the sun too long.

He asked me about my recollections and how it was that I survived. I can remember thinking that this was a strange enquiry to make as it all seemed quite straight forward to me. I told him that I had fallen into a large hollow, hit my head, and when I awakened my head hurt, as did my ankle. All very simple really. He appeared fascinated by the scar upon my head and even more so about where the accident took place. He seemed to want to know every detail of the hollow and how I got there. He asked about the ruin and the flora and fauna surrounding it.

Upon mentioning the whereabouts of it I thought I saw a look of concern in amongst the fascination. He muttered to himself, none of his exclamations made any sense to me. Although his hands were cold, he was not devoid of warmth as he was to demonstrate shortly before leaving my bedside. He gave me an amulet and instructed that I keep it upon my person. It would make me feel better, or so he said. The Doctor instructed me to keep this gift a secret and forbade me to tell anyone about the it. He told me not to worry but never to go off searching for the place again.

It was not a handsome thing he gave me; a crudely cut gemstone, a small bone and few feathers, held together by a coarse binding of copper wire. Why a man of science gave me such a thing I have no idea, it seemed too elaborate for a placebo alone. Whatever it was, I am sure it was given to reassure a small child; an object to cling to if, and when, troubled by nightmares or recurrence of pain. And I did have nightmares, though I cannot recall holding this awkward looking object close to me. I guess I was too scared my parents would see it. For years it remained hidden away underneath the bottom drawer of my bedside cupboard. Many of my dreams consisted of seeing myself at the place of my accident, looking down upon my body and watching the onset of leaves falling about my person.

I suppose I dealt with all these things by making a world of my own. Thankfully my imagination served me well as I often played by myself. I think I was a fairly contented child, though looking back, was never able to rid myself of the tingle of unease I then felt. Most of this I believed stemmed from this imaginary friend that watched over me, except he (I can only assume it is a he) was not really a friend, more of an unbidden companion. As an adult, I know such instances of imaginary friends are not uncommon, and why should they be? I would have loved to have a pal to chase away the birds and build castles of mud with. This kind of friend, I am told, is largely conjured up at will. This one was not.

I once asked my sister Ann about the possibility of a twin. She dismissed the idea outright, though amusing herself for a while by teasing me about it afterwards. She also queried my reasoning, by asking why my parents would have given away my supposed twin. Ann always was riddled with common sense.

Unlike the others, she was more sympathetic towards me than anyone else after my accident. I think it shocked her, and if she was honest, I think she too believed me dead and buried. Like my parents, she chose to think that I had been taken in by someone and nursed back to health, but I could not recall it. It was the easy option to believe and to them the most plausible. I had frequent bouts of amnesia after the fall, but I am convinced to this day that there was no change of location from where I fell to whence, I was awoken. Young boys at this age are inclined to doubt very little, but indirectly I was forced to doubt much. To this day it perplexes me, but a lifetime of invention?

Chapter 12

Black Spot and Greenfly - Part of a letter from Adam to his sister Ann

I hope all is well with Matthew and yourself. I am glad your mine is still turning a shilling. You really must get me something fashioned out of jet seeing as you have so much of it - cufflinks, or maybe a pin for my cravat perhaps? Mrs McCreedie, the new housekeeper, is settling in well. She seems a good stick, but I doubt she will be as able as Dorothy, but then who could be?

All is well here; at least nothing has fallen, though most of the upstairs windows are in a poor state of repair. Do not fret, though. I will get someone in to sort it when I have a moment free. I am still having much success with my plants. You really must see the latest rambling rose we have produced. We are to call it "Walter's Claret" after Grampa's love of the stuff. Both bloom and rootstock were created here by Tom and I. Such is the strength and longevity of this rose, I have cleared all of the old ramblers on the west side of the house and replaced them with these. We left the white climbing rose mother planted, as we felt the contrast would look most becoming. The red rose's flower is devastating; in shade it sulks to the darkest scarlet, though in full sun it transcends to exuberant blood red. It flowers non-stop for at least two months of the year and as yet seems utterly free of both black spot and greenfly. Its scent is incomparably glorious, a joy to embrace; the elusive bewitchment of an old rose, yet none of their frailties. Its magnificence broods upon me as a willow would a stream. And there are many others, not just roses, that are equally resplendent.

Alas, the same cannot be said about yours truly. Despite all of my optimism and passion I seem to be suffering from a lack of vigour, which is a blasted nuisance. I have not felt up to venturing into the village much lately either. Mrs McCreedie orders everything I need as regards the supplies, so that is not a problem. My doctor seems to be at a loss as to the provenance of this dissipation. Of course, he suggests a break by the sea, rest and a little brandy before bedtime as they all do. I do believe that if my bedtime gets any earlier, I shall be meeting myself getting up. Hopefully, it will right itself in the end. I have taken him up on the brandy of course, and no, that is not why I am going to bed early.

I cannot say I am missing going into the village either. The last few times I ventured there I sensed a change in people's regard for me. It is as though my presence raises some sort of alarm amongst them. It makes me anxious, if I am honest. Even old Fanny Dodwell crossed the road when she saw me coming. Frank Potter at the tobacconist seemed spare of conversation too, which as you know is almost inconceivable. A few people have asked me about how things are going but avoided my gaze. I am sure it is not just me, something has changed, and I do not know what.

One last thing, when I was going through my old things the other day, I came across the strange amulet I was given years ago. Do you remember it? I cannot recall if I told you about it or not. Dr Tewson gave it to me after my fall; told me to keep it a secret. I presumed it had been lost when we moved back to this country.

Chapter 13

Absorption - Diary extract

I have always thought of myself as having a keen sense of smell, though now it has reached unenviable heights. As soon as I enter a room, I am immediately arrested by the scents within. When exposed to anything but the faintest of smells they colour my every thought and emotion, flooding my senses with information, place, purpose and disposition. At times I have been so overwhelmed that I have had to take my leave of certain locations. Of course, there are instances where one would willingly drown in the elusive beauty of a scent, but alas these are few and far between. Every smell encapsulates a story, I suppose, and many provoke response, no matter how infinitesimal or subtle the scent. For good or ill, I am now exceedingly well read upon the perfumes of life.

Not only have I been whisked up some ghastly paths by these odours, I now seem to be a catalyst for such forays. Evidently, I appear to be literally soaking up scents. A disposition which I have labelled *reciprocation.* It is as though I have become a human sponge. Some people have recently remarked that I have taken on the scent of flowers, herbs and even perfumes worn by others that I have shared a room with. Mrs McCreedie now informs me what plants I have been working with that day unless they have been virtually odourless. I find this baffling as I have always been a stickler for washing and ridding myself of my work clothes when finishing my tasks.

Alas this is not the only form of absorption that I am having to endure. I believe the *other* seeks to get ever closer. At first, I believed the voices I began to hear were no less than projections of my inner doubts, brought on by fatigue and lack of sleep. Words and sentences, at times disassembled, disjointed and dissociated from rhyme or reason. Half perceived whispers for the most part, but not always…Sometimes I actually think this thing is trying to converse with me. Once or twice I swear that I have heard it call out my name. I also now hear other sounds around me which should not be there. Noises I cannot account for, a creak here, a rattle there. Nothing I can readily pin down exactly. I sense a threat and remain forever watchful.

Chapter 14

Abundant Crop

"I have never seen anything like it!" Tom's wife exclaimed.

"I told you that you wouldn't have. See I have not been exaggerating."

"Just look at those oranges. And that old lemon tree."

"I know, I know. We shall have to cut it back soon. We had the man round from the Botanical Gardens in Oxford yesterday. I could tell he was amazed at what is happening. A little jealous too, I reckon," Tom said with a wink.

"We must go there again soon, Tom. We ain't been since we were a-courting."

"Reckon that is true, Molly. Well, we may well get a chance. From what Adam told me they want a few of the specimens moved over there. I will see if there is room on the cart for us."

"I would like that. No wonder they want 'em. If there is any of those Sevilles begging I could make some lovely marmalade out of those oranges."

"Oh I am sure he could spare us some,"

"Never seen a crop like it, Tom. Tell Adam I will make him some too - as many pots as he can eat."

"You can tell him yourself, he is here now." Tom knew Adam was on the way as he heard the scrunch of the flints upon the path. "There he is. I told you."

"Good afternoon to you both," Adam said upon opening the door of the citrus house, before lifting up his walking stick and smiling. "I don't know, Tom. I thought you would have seen enough of the place, let alone dragging your lady wife with you."

"It is a pleasure to pop in and see what adventures you two have been up to. He is always going on about what is going on in the greenhouses and the grounds," replied Molly.

"I see, well yes, we have been in luck recently. Have you shown your good lady the orchid house yet?"

"Not yet, I shall do presently though."

"Mark that you do. There are some beautiful specimens in there."

"Molly here was wondering if she could steal a few of those Sevilles over there to make some marmalade with?"

"Tom!" Molly said poking him in ribs.

"Ha, why yes of course. Have as many as you like. Mrs McCreedie has already had some for that very reason."

"I will be sure to give you a pot or two, Mr Cuttlebrook."

"Call me Adam, Molly please. Yes, I would like that."

"Thank you for that, Mr... Adam."

"She would put anything in a jar that one. Put me in one too if she could find one big enough, I am sure, always pickling," Tom interjected with mischief.

"Shhh now, you big oaf," Molly replied with mock severity.

"Well, Molly, Tom and I spend a lot of time behind glass, so I guess we are half way to being pickled already ha ha. Now you will have to excuse me," said Adam, dry mouthed, and stifling a cough. "Remember the orchid house, Tom. Good day to you both."

"I will,"

"Cheerio," Molly smiled and waved goodbye. "He don't look too well to me, poor bugger. It was as much as he could do to open that door did you see?"

"That door does get a little stuck mind, but you are right, he has not been that good for a while now."

Once outside, Adam breathed a vast gulp of cool air and waved at the couple. No longer could he endure the heady scent of the citrus house for long despite the clement company and the elegance therein.

"I never knew he used a walking stick?" Molly enquired.

"He has only just started using it. Told me the weather was affecting an old ankle injury of his."

"Hmm, bless him. He looks more like fifty than thirty don't he; nervous with it, too?"

"Maybe so, dear. Come on, enough of that, let's go see those orchids he wanted you to see."

Chapter 15

The Ghost - Diary extract

I have never been one to need much sleep but now it brings me so little comfort that I try to avoid it completely. Despite my sister's denial, I still wonder whether I have a twin, an evil twin at that.

Chapter 16

Feline

"Good god what a sight! What the devil happened here?"

"Looks like the doings of a lunatic."

"That is what I said to the Sarge, but they reckon not."

"Not! Are you saying they are the work of a sane man?"

"No, not at all. Apparently, it is not the work of a person at all. They reckon she was attacked by a big cat, a lion or leopard, that sort of thing."

"I see,"

"They are trying to get an expert down from Oxford to find out what exactly caused this."

"Thank you, Palmer. Not that it will make much difference to this poor wretch."

"Her name was Mrs Limmings, on her way to a neighbour's. Took a short cut across the green and… well, you can see what became of her."

"I can, and I suppose no one saw this beast on the prowl?"

"No one at all."

"Some madman is behind this, Palmer. This incident should not be taken in isolation. When this so-called *expert* arrives from Oxford, ask him if he knows anyone locally with a collection of exotic animals. I wager one of them is behind this, if not, they are aiding and abetting the real culprit. The creatures are just doing what nature intended, same cannot be said of the man or woman responsible for this. They must be fleet of foot and know the area well for them not to have been seen. Cunning and patient too, biding their time for the opportunity to present itself. These deaths are related and deliberate, mark my words."

"Jemmet then?"

"I am not sure; he is a killer, a clever one too. He made sure not to kill his victims in the same way, that is true. Whether that was done on purpose, I cannot say. He started out petty pilfering, then burglary; houses and farms mainly. Much as it loathes me to say it, he was good at it, too. He would have got away with it had he not killed that farmer, Pullen, from out Attingdon way. That turned the whole place against him. Then he went on to kill again."

"The man does not lack for cunning then, sir, but where would he keep such a creature?"

"Creatures, I think you mean."

"Do you think he has more than one of these vicious cats?"

"Possibly, though not just cats. I doubt whoever it is is acting alone. It is plausible he has some sort of hold on one of these landed types with a menagerie. Maybe one of them is harbouring him. Not out of choice but, you never know, I suppose."

"He knows the lay of the land, and the people in it. If anyone could vanish into a hedgerow, it would be him; short fellow, agile, too."

"Though, as far as we know, nothing has been stolen yet in this spate of deaths."

"So, it would seem. These must be revenge killings, but why be so elaborate? Big cats, birds, bees maybe even a snake, for god sake. I want you to tell Sergeant Dickens to make plans to search the grounds of every manor house within five miles of the village; large farms too. If there is even a whiff of a menagerie, I want a complete house search too, do you hear me?"

"Right you are, sir, though that could take some time."

Chapter 17

The Fisherman's Inn

"Evening, Archie,"

"Good evening to you, Arnold. The usual is it?"

"Yep but bung a whisky chaser to keep it company."

"Coming up."

"Not playing Aunt Sally today then, boys?" Joked Arnold.

"No, I am not for sure. Too bloomin' cold for that, Archie. Besides, the river is up again, the grass is too soggy."

"I should say so. Looks like I will have to suffer your company again then, ha."

"Looks as like,"

"What's new then, boys?"

"Not much. Bob was just on about the Cuttlebrook place, up Shabbington House."

"I see. Do tell."

"There is something not right about that young Cuttlebrook fellow up there."

"Oh, you are not still going on about him being seen walking the lanes again, accusing him of murder?"

"I am not accusing him of nothing, though old Granny Robinson was sure she saw him on the common around the time of Mrs Limming's death."

"But everyone knows that was done by a wild beast of sorts, probably escaped from a bloody circus. Either that or Wynn's dog got him. Bloody thing should have been put down years ago. You saying he is a werewolf? Ha ha."

"Of course not. I am just saying there is something odd about what is going on up there. Everything is growing out of proportion up there. It's not right..."

"How much of that ale have you had, Wiggins? You are always exaggerating, man. If anyone is out of proportion it is you, old boy. Look at the size of you."

"Very funny. It is true, I tell you. I have looked over the hedge at the shrubbery. It is as though the grounds are being devoured by its own garden."

"Same could be said about the nettles on your allotment, could they not?"

"It is not the same and you know it. It's looking like a jungle."

"Aww well, that is where he used to live so maybe he is at home with that. It was never like that when Lu was calling the shots; it was a picture."

"It was, yes. Mind you, it was always a good bit of ground, that. Best strawberries for miles. Best in Buckinghamshire I would say, and Oxfordshire, for that matter."

"See; the answer lays in the soil."

"Bah, think what you like, I tell you there's something not right about it."

Chapter 18

A Calling

"Good morning to you, Inspector Clements."

"You too, Mr Cuttlebrook."

"Pleasure to see you in Shabbington House. We do not often see you around these parts."

"Er no, have not had much call since your late father and Lu passed away. No fêtes on the lawn any more?"

"Ahh, I see; yes, I had been thinking about that. Maybe I should revive that tradition. It is just that I have been so… busy of late. You think it would be a good idea, then?"

"Well, it would not be for me to say, though I can see it would improve relations between you and the village folk."

"Relations… I was not aware there was any bad feeling in the village against us," Cuttlebrook lied, and continued, "We have always supported them in every way possible. Are you saying they have taken umbrage at me for no longer holding the fête?"

"No, no, I am not saying that at all."

"Then forgive me, what are you saying, Inspector?" Adam replied, less politely than he wished.

"These deaths occurring in and around the village are making people nervous."

"Surely you do not suspect that I or any of my staff are involved in such crimes?"

"No, of course not. I am just making enquiries, doing my job."

"I see. Well, feel free to ask away. My staff and I would be happy to help in such matters, though forgive me, you still have not elaborated as to what difficulties there are between us and the villagers."

"Oh, I don't know, more...tittle tattle than anything else. You know how villages are at the best of times, and this clearly is not the best of times. People want answers, and are quick to point the finger of suspicion whether it be deserved or undeserved."

"Hmm, so I am a suspect then?" Adam gave a laugh, albeit a bitter one.

"Everyone is at present, sir. That is the point. Now, if you would not mind telling me where you were on these dates?"

Inspector Clements presented Adam with all of the dates upon which the deaths had occurred. Adam excused himself from the room and went to fetch his diary from upstairs. The Inspector noticed how ponderous Adam was in his movements, if not his mind. Physically, he reckoned Adam to be far older than his years judging by the slow plod of footsteps

71

upon the stairs. Some minutes later, Adam returned with his ample diary. Clements was unsurprised when Cuttlebrook showed him evidence of his whereabouts on all of the dates mentioned. He would, however, have to check out the witnesses to the fact but he seemed of little doubt that Adam was innocent.

"Thank you, Mr Cuttlebrook. I knew there would be nothing in it. Sorry to have troubled you. By the way, do you have, or know anyone that has, creatures of … how shall I put it, an exotic nature?"

"The only exotic creatures I know are Mr Kelly's wife and Flufftop over there." The Sergeant rolled his eyes and looked towards the fat, champagne coloured cat licking its paws by the oven. "As for any of my neighbours, let me think. I do believe the Richards of Worminghall Manor used to have a panther or two, as well as parrots and a few other things. It is some time since I went up that way, though. There are some people in Oxford with vast menageries which they brought back from their travels. I think one of the Universities has a good collection, too."

"I see," the officer sighed in resignation; deflated at the lack of simplicity of the task ahead.

"You are welcome to search the grounds here, though, if you wish. If you can catch one of the pheasants, you are welcome to it. I have no gamekeeper at present and they have gone quite wild, quite wild indeed."

"That is most kind of you, thank you. I shall bear that in mind. Though it would not do for me to be seen taking gifts from folk. Especially from a suspect. I knew there would be nothing in it."

"In what?" Adam queried. The Inspector had turned to leave, and already had a foot outside the door when the question was launched. He could not pretend he had not heard it and chided himself for his loose lips. Obligated to answer he replied,

"Well..." he stammered. Then, breathing heavily, continued, "It is not something I ever gave credence too, but a couple of village folk told me that you were seen on the nights of some of these unfortunate deaths. Not one of these sightings were from...how shall I say it...reliable witnesses; the usual troublemakers. You were not the only person though. There is even talk of witches being behind it. Imagine that! Here we are nearing the dawn of the 20th century and people still believe in witches."

"Whatever next?" Adam replied thoughtfully. "I see. Forgive me if I am wrong. From what I heard, most of these deaths were not actually murders at all?"

"In truth we cannot be sure of anything right now. No incident was the same as the last. Rest assured though, we shall sort it."

"Is that prisoner still on the run? Jemmet is it not? His family still live in Shabbington don't they? A murderer too."

"He is sadly, yes, and yes some of the family still reside in the village. We shall catch him. We have had a few possible sightings, mercifully none close to the village. Given your family's past with this fellow, I would see to it that your doors and windows are locked, as a precaution like. Oh, and if you see anything suspicious be sure to drop by the station house."

"You can count on me, Inspector. Good day to you."

"Good day to you too, Mr Cuttlebrook."

Chapter 19

Out of House and Home - a letter from Ann

Greetings to you, Brother.

As you have guessed, Matthew and I are now back in Whitby. The weather here is bright, though the wind cuts through me like a knife. It was good to see you at the weekend and have a walk around the old place; pity to see the church and some parts of the house in such disrepair. I fear you are neglecting your duties, and yourself, if I am honest. Do get Doctor Griffith back to see you.

I have instructed Mrs McCreedie to feed you up. She assured me that she cooks a large supper every day, but you seldom eat it all, if any. And lay off the spirits, especially as you are not eating sufficiently. Last, but not least, do be on the look-out for Jemmet. He has no love for our family. As you know our father had to get rid of those Jemmets years ago. Old man Jemmet was such an idle beggar. The family never forgave us for the loss of their tied cottage. They always were a bad lot and the son the worst of them all. Get yourself a dog, Adam. It would give you some protection and companionship. Much more than

Flufftop does. All she is likely to do is eat you out of house and home and leave fluff all over the place.

Warmest wishes,
your loving sister,
Ann X

Chapter 20

Looming - Diary extract

Until this dreadful malaise which afflicts me abates, I have decided to focus on building terrarium gardens inside my home. Whether I sell them, or they become my companions I neither care, nor know not at present. Their minute worlds mirror my own enclosure. Although I grow weaker by the day, oddly, I still feel the need to nurture and spread. There is not a lot of light in my world, so I have to be selective about what I allow in. The outer world closes in upon me. I feel the *other's* hand on the loom, spinning; entwining our worlds forever closer, yet I find myself unravelling with doubt.

Chapter 21

Sunset

Adam gazed bleary eyed at the fading of the day. As the sun became blooded so, too, did the surrounding wisps of clouds that danced before it. The great disc was sinking into the embrace of the leafless trees on the distant horizon. Their skeletons black atop the distant mounds of Chilton Hills. Adam heard the whispers of the clouds of the sky. Their voices simpering in secret tongues, an uninvited liaison. Adam was bewildered. The distinction between night and day, summer and winter, life and death seemed unclear. Parallels of his inner and outer world ran into one another. No longer separate. Interwoven, their threads frayed, the edges torn and knotted.

The clouds multiplied within the portrait of Adam's window. Their breadth yawned unmolested across the wide ocean of the above. He regarded their spread with jealous eyes. Beyond each and every one, lay something new, unseen; an unexplored island upon which to tread.

"Not that I shall tread far now," he sighed, eyelids heavy with the exhaustion of thought.

As soon as his eyes shut, he became aware that he was no longer alone in the room. Had Flufftop returned? The idea pleased him. She had been his companion in the house since his return, though she'd disappeared out of the blue two weeks previous. It was no cat. It was not something he had seen or heard before, yet he knew it. Knew it existed that is and attached to him. *At last it has emerged out of the depths of my mind into the house. Did the door open?* He could not be sure. Just as he could not be sure he had closed it? *It must be open now* he thought as a barrel full of air shot through his hair. *The top of my hands are colder now, but how long has it been since I knew them warm? I cannot remember any movement of air like this before.* The room still held an ember of light gifted by the falling sun.

Should I get the lamp? Can I get the lamp? I think I know where it is but where are the matches to light it? There is no need to see with whom, or what, I share this space. Adam was convinced it was the same presence he had known since his youth. Then it was little more than a notion, now he suspected it was almost fully formed, wretched and real. He was in little doubt that the oneness he had known in the greenhouse acted as a portal for this thing to emerge. A malignant seed that grew both inside and outside of him.

In the distance Adam heard the sounds of dogs, not one or two, but a pack, their wails rising and falling in the undulations of the landscape. This would have intrigued him had he not been seized by an immediate sense of foreboding. He sensed the *other* in the room was making its way towards him. He instinctively knew what it would do before he heard the soft footfalls drawing near. *Breath! ... It now has breath; manifested.*

The room became starved of all but the merest whisper of light causing Adam to reflect, *Are the nights growing longer? Is winter upon us?* Oblivious to everything other than the enquiry and the being behind him.

"Are you ready, Adam?" The *other* spoke. At least Adam thought it did. Its utterance broken and abrasive though limpid enough for him to decipher. He shuddered, mortified at the actuality of a voice. *Maybe if I ignore it, it will pass? It is feeding upon me, becoming strong as I grow weak.*

"Do you know how long I have waited for this…. Reclamation?"

Adam was confused by the question and the rasping voice. It sounded much like how he imagined as he himself would have done. He tentatively tried to rise but found it too much effort. *I will not bow to this intruder.* Before him the sun collapsed into the soft mounds of mother earth, sated. A scarlet blush hung upon the horizon; a languid sigh. A memory of youth. There was an intake of breath behind him.

"We are alone in the dark again. We have not been this close in… how many years is it now? Since…the day we parted. Though you never really left me, did you? Although unbound we were yet shackled; bound for life; your life. For it is your life… that I seek."

Adam's fingers tightened upon the arms of the chair. He felt the oak under his fingertips. How solid and true it was. *I will not yield. I shall wait and watch, as if the words were not real, only in my head.* As he listened, the room transformed itself around him. Out of the darkness came birdsong, the beat of wings, the scent of creatures and mud, flooding through the parched and barren land of his senses. He had returned to the hollow, to the heat of Ceylon. His awareness bristled; a web of expectation spun around him. *Are these my own thoughts or that of the other; the ghost?* He perceived something brush up against the back of his chair. There was no reason for him to see what the object was, for he knew it to be a hand.

Although it was not touching his jacket, the area around where the pressure lay became cold. He felt a shallow pulse emanating from the top of the chair. The air moved behind him. Another hand was set upon the chair. A spasm skewered through him; the other hand as cold as the first. Adam's hairs rose in fright at the unseen being lurking behind him. The sound of fingers rustling upon the velvet head of the seat caused his neck and shoulders to tighten. He squirmed as a couple of icy fingers embraced his back, gnawing at the timbre of his being. A vile parchment of air groaned from its mouth. A frozen finger-tip was placed up the nape of his naked neck.

"Ahhhh it is good to feel that skin again."
The stench of its breath revolted Adam. He had smelt that odour before in the jungle. It was the odour of death and decay that hung over the carcasses.

Adam sought to rid himself from the assault upon his nostrils, picturing the beautiful butterfly that he had followed through the jungle; its colours dancing over its wings....*I wonder how many days did I actually lie there? Perhaps my sister has replied to my letter. She would know. When did I check the post last? I cannot be sure. Just as I do not recall the number of days and nights that I lay stiff and motionless in that gaping hole. It was as though I was a chrysalis, waiting for my eclosion, a resurrection. From that moment onwards I could become the many, not just the one, the human one.*

"Oh, but you flatter yourself," the voice uttered, louder than before; withering. The reek of its emission brought Adam's attention back to the *other* in the room, and its finger on his neck. "You may have been able to imagine you can be other things, other beings, feel them even, but you cannot *be* them. To manifest as they are is quite different. That... *pleasure* has been my world and mine alone, until...that is... now." The words were vengeful, brimming with hate. Adam's eyes slid to one side. *I can be other things, I know I can, but it knows me as I know it. It is aware of my thoughts. We may be bound but it cannot know all... the silent pages of my life, the chapters not written, yet alone expressed.* His chest burned with fear. The sheer familiarity of the voice savaged his resolve.

The *others* touch upon his neck was displaced, though the chill remained. *It is on the move.* Adam sensed it would act now. He stole one of his hands from the arm of the chair towards his jacket pocket, sighing inwardly as he felt the bone-handled pen-knife. All illusions of the jungle disappeared; not so the sound of the once distant hounds. *They are close now, upon my land, what has provoked them so? I cannot think...Jemmet! Could it be?* Adam was emboldened by the notion that it may be Jemmet with whom he shared the room, and not any ghostly *other* or malevolent twin.

"Show yourself!" Adam demanded, struggling to gain a mastery over the situation. There was a muffled sound to his rear, breath was exhaled, laboured by movement. *Perhaps he has been shot, injured perhaps; the dogs smell his blood?*
This may be my only chance. He tried to stand but failed. Hunching up, he imagined blows about to rain down upon his head. No blows fell. The agony of the unseen foe prompted Adam to yell,

"Face me, you devil!" the words tore from his body with such anguish it ripped through his lungs causing him to cough violently. There was a rush of air behind him. *Has he fled? Perhaps the police have arrived?* A shred of hope ploughed through the fallow field of his mind.

He heard a floorboard creak above the cry of the hounds. He knew exactly where the board was. *It has not left. It is still here, encased with me.* Another board groaned as the thing he was convinced he shared the house with emerged. Adam thought he could detect a sneer. *It cannot be,* he squirmed. *It must be the scarcity of light playing tricks upon me. I see me. It is me, half formed.* Adam blinked but the vision remained, twisting and turning, the outline of its features lit with a vaporous light. Its face ebbed back and forth; pallor of arsenic, white, bloodless. The seated man sought focus upon the *other* while attempting to pull the now opened blade from his pocket.

"Tell me, what do you see?" the apparition croaked.

"I...I am not sure what I see. Do you know what I see, do you know yourself?" Adam answered, his words terse and tight within his throat.

"Oh,...I am well aware of what I am, and whom I shall become. It is you that are not aware of what, or who, you are."

My mind has abandoned me, surely. This thing cannot be real. It is Jemmet, playing tricks. Yes, that is what it is. He is torturing me. He must be wearing a mask to look like me. Why did Clements not tell me what he looked like? Perhaps he is in on it, too?

The vacillating form remained out of Adam's reach. *Just one step forward. I may stand a chance, if I could just stand...*

"Very well then," the intruder stepped forward. Adam flinched, unable make sense of what he saw.

"I see you recognised me,"

"But...what I see is...," Adam whispered.

"Indeed...it is so. As you see, I am now no longer much of what you would call 'a ghost'. Soon I will be complete and will not have to suffer such an imposition much longer. I will be re-formed. I shall reclaim myself, and *you* will vanish forever, back to the stinking jungle where you belong, back to the worms."

"Your body?" His response was no more than a reflex of disbelief. "It cannot be, you are Jemmet, or my vile twin." *My sister must have lied.*

"Ha ha ha! Your twin indeed. You stole what was not yours. I have watched over you since you took what was mine in the jungle. I could never quite reach you before; never thought I could until...until you reached outside of yourself. Before that I could not be...whole, I could never...manifest. Your loss of self made you weak and soon I found that death gave me power. You were born out of my demise, and I would use that power of death against you. Think of it as a kind of photosynthesis, plants-man. Now you are weak, and I am strong." A dreadful image flashed through Adam's mind. That of the hungry pitcher plant, its prey tumbling into its vast hollow... disintegration...

"It was you that killed all of those people," Adam yelled, knowing the answer before it was delivered.

"Oh, yes. Impressive, don't you think? Firstly, I did it just to find out if it were possible. I have learnt that everything feeds on something. When I realised that I could, and not only could, it gave me energy as well, I continued. I was not greedy though; unlike you. I enjoyed that my true form came back however fleetingly, and you became a suspect. The swarm of bees was interesting...how they can all act under one mind, one purpose. Sadly, I could never hold any of my forms long though. Unlike my flesh, my power *did* return. I knew that I could not attain a wholeness again until I had taken your life; your false life. See how just being close to you makes me stronger."

"My life?" Adam replied, still utterly confused as to whom he was addressing.

"Yes. There cannot be two of us. You are the imposter, a mere changeling of the woods. I bided my time, I watched the other creatures and plants in the jungle. I ran with them, I flew with them, I crawled with them until... I could be one of them. I had no form, no constraints, you see. This, I feared, was all I could ever be until you began to mimic me. So you see, it was *you* that lead me back into the world of substance and form," the *other* spat.

Adam gripped the knife tight.
"You are nothing more than a foul product of my imagination, a sickness."

He was convinced he saw a baleful grin creeping upon the face of the intruder. A hideous peal of laughter rang through the room, booming out around the house, over the fields and into the distant village beyond.

"Is that so? And yet you dare not stand and face me. I am much more powerful than you are now and yet I am not fully formed." A loud thump came from below stairs. *The hounds are in the house. It must be Jemmet here. It must.* Adam heaved himself up from the chair, mustering every drop of energy left in him. He drew his knife; thrust it towards the shadowy figure before him. Just as it was about to be buried into the chest of the sneering *other,* he halted. Transfixed by the empty, malevolent eyes before him.

"Allow me," whispered the *other.* At least, that is what Adam thought he heard. The *other* made a grab for the blade. Adam fought for control, and as he did so he imagined the butterfly he followed in the jungle. How it swam through the air, evading all in his way. He stepped back as the knife slashed through air and ripped into Adam's shirt. The amulet, given to him in Ceylon, hung around his neck, exposed. The room became awash with the scent of cinnamon. Hounds feverishly pounded up the stairs. A shriek of anguish pierced the room's shell where the struggle had taken place. Recognition. Solitary footsteps tore across the landing. Hounds now engulfed the house. The door was flung open and a ravaged man entered; his clothes filthy, no more than rags hanging off his skeletal frame. Wizened as he was, he still had the countenance of a feral beast. Exhausted, he halted, reached into his pocket, sucking in great gulps of air. Men shouted from upon the stairs, hounds now threading through the landing.

The man in the doorway shouted, "Never again shall a Cuttlebrook take away a Jemmet's home!" as the figure by the window raised his hands in appeasement. Dogs burst in, tearing at the leg of the ragged man. A shot rang out, then another. To anyone not a witness to the scene, it would sound as though only one bullet was loosed, the second a mere echo of the first.

Blood gushed from the back of Jemmet's head, as he sank to his knees, gun in hand, lost in a clammer of hounds. The policeman who fired the second shot ran past Jemmet towards the shadowy figure by the window. This form seemed to be clutching his chest as he stared at the policeman in horror before toppling through the pane of glass behind him.

Chapter 22

An unopened birthday card, (delivered on the day of the shootings, addressed to Adam Cuttlebrook, from his sister, Ann)

Happy birthday, Brother.

You will soon be catching up on me ha ha. Let us see. How old are you now?

I am sorry you have had to let the housekeeper go. What was the matter with her? I hope you did not upset the poor woman. Have you had the Dr back around to see you again?

In answer to your questions: I do not know exactly how many days you were missing, though mother always said it was well over a month. God only knows how you survived. Everyone thought you had been savaged or kidnapped. I know you will not give the idea any credence, but I suspect you were taken in by someone. You have just forgotten about it, I am sure. There is no other explanation for how you survived. It is a mystery really, is it not?

Sorry I forgot to tell you this in my last letter. I do not recall you showing me any amulet, but I do remember Doctor Tewson. How could I forget?

Strange little man. His hands were always freezing cold. Father and mother always called him the witch Doctor, now I know why.

Please do take better care of yourself. We all want you well again. Besides, you have your seeds to sow, do you not?

I hope you like your present. For the life of me, I have no idea why I have never shown you this before. Anyway, it is yours now. I know you will take care of it, if nothing else. I brought the butterfly back with me from Ceylon when we left. Isn't it amazing how it has maintained its beautiful colours after all these years behind the glass? No one has managed to name it yet. Perhaps you can.

Many Happy Returns,
Ann X

What Milky Darkness

What milky darkness your presence conjures up,
Wrapped in your coat of ill definition,
Beguiled by the flames of mortal superstition,

Drunken spirals fall,
Tawny, black, grey, mottled, be-speckled, De-
Jekelled.
Dreaded in all,

Under slate, under side, out from under a warm divide
In porch and post lies a succulent host,
Unwanted wings from moss and cold moor,
Spinning through your front door,

Cloaked in timber, cloaked in wall,
Watch how they do circle around your hall,
All your Jekylls hide, forbidden Hyde,

Arisen from the prism of dark ill-wrought dreams,
Be-winged dark stars of nocturnal edge,
Sidling and jumping through unbridled hedge.
Into your home unbidden, forbidden,

Silent is the prowler at the gates of your mind,
Making its nest where you'll never find,
Hoary silks it does weave,
Devouring its host you had better believe,

Time will tell whether it stays with you until the day
does drown?
Or whether it chooses to rest in your gown…

To Each His Own

"Let's hope those Mackerel are biting today,"
"It is a bit late in the season, but Alan one-eye
reckons there were plenty in the Pembroke harbour
last night."
"Well we'll soon find out."
The three men had been planning a day's fishing off
the rocks since early summer, but up until now the
weather, work and other commitments had scuppered
their plans. It was now mid-September and the flare
of the Autumn light spread richly and deep upon the
hedgerows. Berries and rose hips hung heavily upon
the dewy briars.

They had not yet encountered any cars since joining
the coastal road, which was just as well as there were
precious few passing points so far. At first the road
meandered along gently; dissecting fields of cows and
sheep baying lazily in the lush pastures. Now,
however, it became a little testy, with steep gradients,
blind bends, and forks in the road, often from
nowhere, seldom marked; anonymous. High hedges
and wizened stands of pine and sycamore masked the
steep cliffs below. Seagulls neither of land or sea
looped languidly on the wing.

The travelling companions mocked one another merrily as the car traversed the ridgeway.

"Come on Michael, put your foot down, don't dawdle," urged Phil from the back seat.

"Don't worry I will," replied Michael, though he had not the least intention of racing along such a precarious track, especially now, as a wall of fog had just pushed in from the seashore.

I seem to remember hating this stretch of the road last time I came, how long ago was that then? Michael asked himself. Preoccupied by the incoming fog Michael slowed the car down drastically, losing almost all the momentum needed for climbing the steep slope before them. Michael rapidly sought out a lower gear. A loud scrunch pealed out across the hillside telling all and sundry that his mission had been successful. The car jerked; a noxious plume of black smoke seeped into the fog, identity lost, swallowed up by its vaporous maw. As they approached the top of the ridgeway Michael saw a dense bone-coloured form emerging out of the fog and sweep of black trees. He was sure he had never encountered a feature of such prominence on his last journey this way. *Am I on the right road? I will never hear the last of this if I am not,* he ruefully thought.

"Wow look at that stone, it's massive, never noticed that before," Phil said in awe from the back seat.

"Nor I, not that I have been here much," Joe concurred.

Michael was relieved he was not the only one.

"That said, I can't say for sure I have been this way before, ha ha," snorted Phil.

"Yes, you have Phil, course you have, you came before…hmmm... I think. I don't know, anyway the driver knows where we are headed don't you, Michael?" Joe said idly.

"Of course," the driver lied. He had incurred such a perfectly cut standing stone before. It almost shone, free from ivy, algae and all other encumbrances of the passage of time

"Maybe that is Brisen's stone. My father used to tell tales about it, not that I can remember any of them now."

"I think it has been on the news before as well," said Phil. "I heard say it was out this way."

"Who the hell is Brisen?" Joe asked.

"She was said to be a famous enchantress from years ago."

"A witch you mean," said Joe snidely.

"I suppose," Phil replied.

"I have known plenty of witches in my time. Perhaps one of them is looking after it," joked Joe.

"Do you reckon it is a magic stone then Phil?" he jested.

"I have heard about it too," Michael intervened, and continued, "It is quite well-known Joe."

"Magic stone my arse, shove it down the bank, let's see if it floats, then we will find out how magical it is; bloody dangerous on that bend."

The driver rolled his eyes; looked in the rear-view mirror once more then back at the stone. The stone had gone.

"Watch out!" someone yelled.

Michael, distracted, swerved and slammed down hard on the brake, too hard.

"Shit" he yelled.

The car veered up a mossy bank and back down again before screeching to a halt.

"What the hell are you doing?"

"Sorry...I... lost concentration and..."

"And you could have killed us all. Do you know how close we are to the cliff?" asked Phil.

"Yes, I do, it was just that...it was just that..."

"Just watch the bloody road,"

"Yes, get a grip Michael."

Michael considered telling them why he'd been distracted but thought better of it. *Where has the stone gone?* The fog lifted behind him and gave him a clear view. He wanted to get out of the car and find out why he could no longer see the giant monolith they had passed. *I had better not, I can imagine what they would say; besides the fog has returned and it is dangerous enough inside the car let alone out of it.* He turned the key, the car's engine started first time. That at least offered some relief.

After a little hesitation he looked in the rear-view mirror and set off once again. Fog came down anew, his vision obscured. The atmosphere inside the car turned sour and silent. Stifled by the nothingness outside, the men's attention turned inwards, and upon each other.

After a short while two beams of light appeared ahead, their stare cold and soulless. Barely visible at first, shrouded by amorphous vapour, they soon widened and bore down with alarming velocity. *They are going to move to one side are they not?* Michael asked himself, terrified by the rapidity of the vehicle's approach. There was no escape; he could not turn off the road or reverse quickly enough to avoid a collision. Pulling to a halt as close to the bank as possible, he blasphemed quietly and waited. "Jesus it's a bloody milk tanker!" Phil yelled, incredulous, the last syllable of his words barely audible, lost in whisper. The huge vehicle sped on heedlessly, showing no regard for the paltry car in front of it.

With a second to spare it swerved clear; its mighty wheels mounting and mashing up the verdant banking, leaving nothing but a trail of bracken, mud and stones in its wake. Through almost closed eyes Michael had glimpsed the face of its driver. A man, early fifties, hair white and unruly. His expression grim, preoccupied; fear resided in his eyes. Michael knew nothing was going to make him slow down.

"The bloke's a lunatic," said Phil.

"What on earth does he think he is doing?" added Joe, before continuing, "you can't drive like that up here."

"You can't," agreed Michael, "you don't, unless …unless you are in a serious hurry to get somewhere or… avoid something."

Michael looked ahead; the road appeared clear of all but the sea's foggy breath. He glanced at his side-view mirror, then the rear before gingerly pulling off.

All clear…But it's not, is it? Something had moved behind but he forced himself not to look. *It was not a car, so it's fine isn't it?* he told himself, without conviction. *Eyes to the front, don't look back.* Despite his best efforts he could not refrain from taking a peep. *It is still there;* his attention strayed from the road and lingered on what he saw behind him. *God, it's a face, it's a bloody face.* He stole his eyes away and stared straight ahead. *Should I tell them? Better not, or they should think me mad. I am not stopping again either, not for hell or high water.*

I swear these great broods of fog coming and going are toying with me deliberately, goading me like a vindictive cat would a mouse. Hark at me, giving this fog a personality, giving it a face. I need to get out of here. It cannot be far now to the crossroads can it? His confidence waned as the car started its descent.

This had better be the right road. I'll know it when I see it I am sure; more of a buzzard's claw than a crossing of roads; sharp and sinewy with a huge oak watching over. It would not surprise me if that tree had been used as gallows years ago, it had that feel about it. A feel of death. The road bulged then tightened, edges made obscure in the hoary breath. Definition gone.

He saw something swoop down behind him. *A bird,* Michael concluded, with more hope than conviction. Blindly, he sought to avoid it, veering across the road. His passengers shouted with alarm. Michael nodded but did not reply. *What a fool I am trying to evade something that lays behind me. I need to see daylight again,* increasing the speed. That which he sought to ignore loomed up upon the rear windscreen once more. *Jesus, it really is a face. It can't be human can it?* He saw the face of an elderly woman. Her head seemed almost fluid to him; falling away then lurching back up, obscenely large and hideous. Michael's shoulders tightened, he was trapped between doubting his own sanity, the scorn of the others, and the terrifying vision behind.

The dreadful apparition had not come alone. It brought with it the smell of fire, a coal fire, sulphurous. And a peculiar hissing sound, of which there seemed no obvious source. Rigid with fear, he inched down the accelerator. *Oh no, you won't catch me, I will out-run you.* His passengers seemed oblivious to the gradual creep of speed that Michael injected. Their attention now diverted by the narrow escape with the tanker, they now made small talk, and fidgeted unnecessarily. As the road continued it deepened significantly; gouging the surface of the

earth's skin.

"Right, this is not a joke, but I just have to say it," Michael spoke directly, though his tone bubbled with emotion. "Look behind you, tell me, what do you see?"

"Fog. There is bloody fog, or mist, or whatever you want to call it everywhere. What sort of question is that?" Aware that Phil had not bothered even to look, Michael instructed him to look once again. This time his voice was firm, urgent.

"Ok, ok, keep your hair on," Phil replied, humouring the driver, casting his gaze behind him. Not even the sedate rise and fall of the windscreen wiper masked what he saw. He gasped and turned around, ashen, his demeanour transformed, beyond recognition.

"Drive, for god sake drive, go, go."

"What the devil has got into you," Joe replied from the front passenger seat scornfully. He too had not previously troubled himself to look.

"Just look why don't you," Michael yelled. Joe cricked his neck trying to look behind him so he looked into the wing mirror instead. His head rocked back in an instant. He shrieked violently, more infant than adult, which caused Michael to stab at the brake. The car snaked across the road narrowly missing a stone wall; a crumbling echo of the previous order along the wayside.

Michael recognized the face in the fog and knew the person to whom it belonged, or once belonged, but he had never seen it so contorted with rage before or swollen full of malice. It was old Meg, the travelling woman he had known since childhood. When passing she had often stayed in a ruined cottage just outside the hamlet where he was born. His brother and he harangued the old woman, stealing her food, and urinating on the glowing embers of her fire when she was out. One night, after he and his brother had been particularly spiteful to her, she was found dead, wrapped up in a threadbare sheet and ripped plastic bags. That was the hiss he heard; steam from her fire. The fire now burned from her eyes penetrating the mist.

Phil still had his head bowed covering his face with his calloused hands. His head shook as if trying to rid himself of some unknown foe. At Michael's side Joe too shook, shifting around in his seat. He had ripped off the top buttons of his shirt and wriggled as if besieged by termites. Eyes wet and wide, tears trickling down his face.

"You see it too, you see her, you see the woman?" Michael asked.

"Just go, go" replied Phil from underneath his clenched hands.

"You too Phil?"

"I see her," he answered, with barely a whisper. Joe opened his window.

"Shut the stench out now," Michael shouted. The further the window was lowered the more overpowering the sulphurous fumes became and the louder the hiss.

"Yes, shut it," Phil shouted from the back, "don't let that stench in."

"Thank god, I thought it was me," Michael exclaimed out loud what he had hoped to keep to himself.

Joe had already started to close the window before the driver requested it. He had become overwhelmed with the scent of patchouli oil; the perfume often worn by Claire, a past girlfriend.

"She is no woman, she's a girl," yelled Phil from the back seat.

"No girl Phil, she is in her thirties," Joe reacted.

"She is eighty if she's a day" Michael interjected incredulously.

"You making fun of her?" Joe asked angrily, knowing full well what a hypocrite he was, having beaten his girlfriend black and blue in a jealous rage many years previously. The bruising on her pale skin as plain as day to him now.

"Turn the fan off, the smell of chlorine is choking me," Phil yelled. He shouted to be heard above the raised voices in the swimming baths where his mind dwelt. Full of remorse and horror at the fun he had had at school; repeatedly holding his classmate Susan's head under the water until she fought for breath. Thrashing around like a kitten in a sack. "She may look eighty, but she is only a child, just ten years of age you idiot!" He screamed at Joe. Joe, unfastening his seat belt, turned to face Phil. He flung a fist at his jaw. Phil retaliated, kicking Joe's hand ferociously. Joe yelped in pain. Unaware that the accelerator pedal was now flat to the floor Michael searched for the old woman behind him. She was nowhere to be seen. *Where is she?* Michael asked himself, his eyes searching every mirror and every window in vain. Joe by this time had turned completely around and was kneeling upon his seat. The two passengers cursed and landed savage and

relentless blows upon each other. Demented by guilt and rage, neither could defeat the other. The past blinded and bound their present. Their future set in stone.

In an instant the fog thinned. Michael inhaled deeply. A swift silence fell upon all inside the vehicle. A ray of sunlight pierced through the trees. Michael noticed something nestling upon the misty patch at the top of the windscreen the wipers never reach. Too thick for a twig and a little too thin to be called a branch. Within a blink of an eye another one appeared with a gentle thud. Slowly they slid down the windscreen. Michael paid them little heed. *The wipers will shift them*, he mused.

The windscreen wipers did not remove them. They continued to make their way down the screen. The farther they slid the more the top end seemed to thicken. The lower end of the woody debris became more clear. Their tips were not blunt. Each possessed five long spindly growths.

"Those aren't twigs," his scream stuck in his throat, as the forms passed through the glass. His mouth remained open; hollow. The lower extremities of these intrusions lunged towards him. They made a cracking as they spread out. Still the scream stuck in Michael's throat. The gnarled fingers crawled across his face towards his neck. Long ashen grey hair blew across his face, eyes flamed ….

South West Wales Gazette

Tragedy upon the Ridgeway

Three local men were killed in a collision at a local accident black spot upon the ridgeway, St Non's Bay, last Tuesday morning. The three were apparently heading out for a day's fishing at Burton Point when tragedy struck. Police believe the car in which they were travelling, left the road shortly after 10 am and collided with a tree known locally as Brisen's Oak. The tree is situated on the cross roads heading towards Miller's Ford, Burton Point and Colliers Way. There have been many calls for this stretch of road to be widened by the public and councillors alike in the past. "Given that there have been numerous fatalities here in the last twenty years, something urgently must be done," said Councillor Lynne Roberts.

It is feared that these recent deaths will only increase the local belief that the road has been cursed since the removal of The Brisen Stone, or Brisen's Stone, which stood at the peak of the ridgeway.

The vast monolith fell into the sea when attempts were being made to move it by the local highway department twenty-one years ago. Police have not ruled out the possibly of one or more vehicles being involved in the incident. Apparently, a number of motorists had already gathered at the scene of the accident before the police and emergency services arrived.

One of which, a Mr Harold Wagerfield of Coopers Hill, Ferryside, tried in vain to resuscitate the driver of the stricken vehicle. None of the motorists questioned appeared to have witnessed the crash itself; though many claimed to have seen a lone female heading away from the site shortly after the incident. As yet, there appears to be no definitive description of the female in question despite many witnesses citing her presence upon the ridgeway. Police have suggested the contradictory nature of the female's description maybe due to the poor visibility of the day.

The Swimmer

Steven looked out of his bedroom window. It was the first dry day of July and he had pledged himself an afternoon off from his drawing board. Since childhood the sea, especially swimming in it, had been a passion of his, though he had often found it difficult to reconcile himself to the fact that the sea was disordered and unpredictable. All of the things he hated.

Despite it being the first day of the school holidays, Steven managed to find a place to park. His bag, which had been packed weeks ago in readiness for such a day, contained two towels, a wet-suit, sun cream and a pair of, as yet unworn, swimming trunks. As he walked along the pathway, across the dunes towards the beach, Steven kept his eyes fixed firmly upon the ground. Just a few years back he had been only a step away from treading on an adder. Although he had since read that the potentially deadly snake would only strike if disturbed, the memory made him shudder.

"You are still out there waiting for me, I know you are, but you will not have me," he whispered softly.

His pace quickened, though the faster he went the less progress he made; footsteps swallowed up by the hungry sand. After much exertion he reached the uppermost bank of the dunes highest and surveyed the bay beneath him. He regarded its mouth with apprehension. *It's smile is an open one but there is something dishonest about it. Perhaps it is the lack of symmetry that gives it such a sneer? It has always been misshapen but today there's something off kilter about it. Maybe it has curdled in the heat?*

The passage through the dunes to the beach was alive with insects, darting hither and thither. The most spectacular of all to him were a cluster of blood red and black moths gorging upon the nectar of a patch of sea-holly. *How oblivious they are to the vindictive sharp spines of their host,* he marvelled.

Although the bay was located upon the far flung, south western reaches of the UK, the beach faced east. Despite it's evident attractions the amount of people choosing to visit this lonely spot remained low. Steven was always puzzled by this and put it down to its remoteness and lack of facilities. As customary, the architect chose a place to set down his towel with care - halfway between the ever-optimistic fishermen angling upon one side of the shore and the motorboats

which buzzed around on the other. He hated the din they made and their intrusive demands on his attention.

Damn things. I don't know how they're allowed to operate here, he thought angrily, flicking away a few pebbles from where the towel was to lie.

Blast! I didn't check the tide times. Now I don't know if the tide is coming in or going out. Judging by that line of dried seaweed ahead of me, my towel should be safe enough. How I hate putting on this wet suit, always such a bloody ordeal, he grumbled fighting with its stifling embrace. *Always feels like the wretched thing is going to squeeze the life out of me.*

Once on, and with the reassuring smell of rubber filling his nostrils, he reached for his sun cream; plastering it over what precious little skin remained uncovered. He knew his eyes would sting viciously when the water ran into them but convinced himself it was worth the pain. Better to remain safe.

There was barely a trace of wind, and not one cloud defaced the perfection of the blue dome above him. The sea too was a lullaby of calm, untroubled and yet for some peculiar reason his mind bent backwards to the adder; biding its time, waiting for his return. It unnerved him and he looked about him cautiously.

There was a small smattering of folk paddling around the sea's edge. They were dotted around the strandline like markers, separating the known world from the unknown one. Some folk were swimming, though not many. Those that were, were no further in than waist height. Further out, small islands of gulls rose and fell upon gentle sway of the water.

It may be baking out here but the sea... Steven winced as his foot entered the great green. *Why does it have to be so painful in here?* he asked himself as his face scrunched up like a paper bag.

"I'll be fine when I get my shoulders under," he whispered, seeking reassurance from within. His body may have hesitated, but his mind was set. Taking great pains to avoid the small pebbles underfoot, he waded outwards. The sea was crystalline, interspersed by golden edged waves, shimmering under the sun's relentless gaze.

Apart from the cold water and the odd stray strand of bladder wrack, the deepening sea welcomed his advances. Something then moved ahead of him. What the...

"Jellyfish!" He yelled and leapt back. Upon a second glance he noted that this particular squidgy invertebrate was quite harmless. *You are undeniably exquisite, fantastic even, but your gelatinous being makes me squirm. Most of you are probably already dead. Those that aren't, soon will be I suspect,* he mused watching them gracefully sail landward, suicidally landward. He paused and imagined himself to be one of their number, without frame, boneless, like the sea itself. Rolling back and forth, with nothing but the moon and the four winds determining their fate. Limb-less and land-less.

He carried that thought seaward, carefully plotting his path through the bloom of pink billowing jellies upon each side. His legs had almost become impervious to the chill now and, if it was not for an icy blade of water stealing its way into his otherwise cold-numbing wetsuit, he was almost at total ease in the great green. Almost; the fear of the serpent remained. It slithered with him throughout every coiled wave. Laughter and the screams of children tore out mockingly from the safe harbour of the shoreline. A few solitary birds flew overhead; none of which were recognizable to him.

Once up to his chest in in the water, he slowly lowered arms into its frigid grasp. He never entered the sea swiftly, especially after having reading how much it could shock one's system. The swimmer splashed the water over himself and shook his arms vigorously, resembling a moth before taking flight.

"It is just about bearable now," he said; urging himself further into the unknown. A wave slightly bigger than the rest approached him. *That's the one I need to get my shoulders under. Once they are under, they shall stay under*. His mother, a non-swimmer, instructed him thus, many years since. Experience proved to him that it was sage advice, as failing to do so meant having to endure the icy chill of submersion all over again.

With reservation he pushed himself backwards into the bulge of the wave as it passed him by. After the initial slap of cold water trickling into his wetsuit abated, he felt liberated and weightless. *Now I am truly as-one with the sea, it is me and I am it*, he reflected, kicking his legs up and down, disfiguring the natural beauty and swell of the water.

He looked behind him, toward the west and the shore. Lines appeared, intersecting the sea from the sand, sand from trees, trees to sky, the empty and formless space above. Shifting in the water he began to swim languidly across the bay towards the northern horizon which was saturated by a blanket of ferns and emerald leaf. He followed the line of the coastal path zigzagging its way up the ragged line of the sandstone cliffs. A peppering of houses clung to their incline, no bigger than barnacles now to Steven's far away eyes.

After an indeterminate amount of time he changed direction, towards the south. *This horizon looks much the same as the northern one except that there is less land, and what profile there is, is decidedly more jagged,* Steven thought, watching its serrated teeth-like rocks rise out of the sea with rude distinction.

"I could do better," he said out loud with his exacting eye. In doing so he let a small slug of seawater into his mouth, which he swiftly spat out. It was not the taste he disliked, in fact it always made him think of fish and chips; it was the possibility that it may be unclean and full of something he didn't know. As the sun ambled its way west, he noticed a flutter of lily-white clouds overhead, their presence emphasising the boundless enormity and freedom that the sky and the sea beneath it offered.

His fingers brushed against something...something unknown. Something of substance, yet not wholly solid. He withdrew in horror, barely able to take a breath. Repulsed, he swam feverishly away from this unwanted touch. The swimmer didn't know in what direction he swam; he just needed to flee from whatever "it" was.

He took some slow deep breaths, seeking to calm himself; to make sense of what it was that he had just encountered. Looking backwards, he hoped to see the 'thing' he had laid his hand upon. The water was still translucent, though he was deeper now and couldn't stand up to see clearly. *Damn, if only I had brought my goggles*, he thought. *Perhaps it was seaweed? Probably, though it felt more... more solid than that. Shark? God, no, it was softer than that. Jellyfish? Possibly.*

It both intrigued and disturbed him in equal measure. He swam again, losing himself once more in the yielding body of water. Catching sight of the shore he turned and swam outwards, towards the east, towards the open sea. There was only one line here: that between sea and the sky. He loved swimming away from the shore; reckoning it profoundly liberating for the soul. And today, he felt that more than ever. Perhaps it was because he was freeing himself from the watchful gaze of the adder or maybe just himself? He didn't know.

"Eyrghhhhh!" he cried out, recoiling. In his panic he swam and swam without once turning around. What the hell is that thing? His heart thumped. His finger's felt the same sensation as before. Instinctively he tried to stand, seeking structure, form. None was to be found this far out.

"Are you following me?" he shouted at the unseen entity. *Maybe it's not the same thing as before, perhaps it's "another?* "What are you?" he challenged the creature to announce itself. He knew his words were wasted, lost amongst the distant roar of the waves. He was now not far away from one of those islands of seagulls. The birds stared at him impassively. *They look upon me as though I'm invisible, transparent, formless.*

A flurry of waves descended upon him. He'd not anticipated their encroachment, his mouth filled with salty water. Spitting it out he saw that the unheralded tremor of water came from a nearby speed boat. It was too distant to pose an immediate physical threat to him, but he still considered it too near. Its irritating sound, must have been lost to him, caught up as he was in his own thoughts. Its hideous noise was all too apparent now. He likened it to that of an angry wasp in need of swatting.

Swimming hastily, he sought to put clear water between himself and the disagreeable vessel. The water seemed colder to him now, and he had become agitated. He didn't know why, but he found himself swimming towards where he'd felt that abhorrent 'something" hidden beneath the surface. As if under an enchantment, he probed the underbelly of the water with his fingers and toes, desperately seeking what he did not know. He neither saw nor felt anything else other than the odd tangle of seaweed, and the occasional pink, almost translucent, jellyfish. None of these felt anything like that of the "other's" touch; they were unfulfilling to him. Besides they were familiar, whereas the other…

A lone oystercatcher hurried past him, paying him no heed whatsoever.

"What are you flying to, my feathered friend?" he asked, snatching a breath as his head rose out of the water.

Inspired by the bird's determined flight, Steven spoke to the thing that teased him so. *I will find you, you there underneath the waves, beneath the surface,* before swimming outwards with enhanced ardour. Out of the corner of his eye he noticed that the sun had inexplicably slipped westward with uncanny haste.

"It doesn't matter," he whispered as his eyes cast out eastwards again, assured that his prey had swum farther out. Onwards he swam, to the line where the sky met the sea. His fingers extending, desperately needing to know its touch; its form once again.

As the heaven's stole into a cloak of teal, Steven eventually laid his fingers upon the elusive something that he believed to be the quarry of his quest. It's substance though, like the fate and form of the wandering architect, remained unknown.

Back upon the dunes however, something watched and waited in silent expectation.

The Mason within a Dreamer

The old house lay, somewhere beyond, beyond, a
boundless property.
Although the house resided in my dreams, it was
never a resident, it was a wayfarer and it did not
belong anywhere at all.
Its knotted timbers were wrinkled, dark and
unyielding.
I entered through many doors and yet I have never
truly left.
There was no fire unto this place; the hearth was
always spare, it bestowed no warmth, though I
shivered not.

The house was set up amidst a wiry concoction of
trees and briars,
Scraggy unnameable growths pencilled high into the
twilight of the canvas.
The house itself has a wealth of inhabitants, yet its
purse was empty.
Long sallow rooms of discontent hide, huddled
between its shadowy eves.
Its neighbours were none; it was solitary, both in
construction and conception.

Although it was not bereft of windows, not once did I venture forth to look out, or anyone engage in looking in.

Its staircases were never lit; I was always blind to my destination, unadvised without charter or quarter.
The air within the dwelling was forever autumnal, as were the creatures, within and without their webs.

Though the house spoke of short days and ceaseless winter it never died.
The house was always alone, singular and unto me, alone.
I cannot remember when it first came unto me?
Perhaps it was before I drew my first breath, I shall never know.

It is neither my sanctuary nor my saviour. Though within its silent passage and passages I roam, alone, un-assailed, unburdened by age or rage.

I can not say whether it possessed memories, if there were any to be found, they were neither mine or thine.

Did I build this solemn place? Or was I shown a version of it so many countless times that I made it my own; mine to build, and rebuild time after time, infinite, indefinite.

With the coming of night, I build a bony skeleton of boards and beams, a vaulted ceiling afresh.

Its once smooth inner skin of lath and plaster, scarred with dry pools of nothingness. Wounds within the walls, its façade of permanence exposed and laid bare. Though it will not die, not even, I suspect, when I go back through the vast gate of making and unmaking.

It shall be either at my side, or this vast and ruinous abode will be bestowed upon another Built with the ragged stone of the moon, the mason within the dreamer.

Arachne

Around and around and around you go
Mistress of the earth I see your delights
Dissolving as I am in your trembling heights,
Wines and dines and finds and binds
There is no confiding in where you are hiding
Lofty spinner of threads and dreads
So softly you tread upon your silken bed
From under step and under stone you crawl and
enthral,
Enthral and crawl and call

As patient as tomorrow, you beg, save and borrow
Crave to enslave, a slave to the grave
From pillar to post your ties are beguiling
Forever a host with no reconciling

You deceive with the finest of weaves,
Strung out on trees there is no reprieve
So good is your suck
So subtle your duct
Quiver oh quiver in your silent embrace
The finest of lace, make haste, give chase
Out of hollow out to bite
Who will be yours on this cold dark night?

The cast of your net
I will never forget
There is wealth in your stealth
And wealth on your shelf
So steal and reveal, unpeel and unpeel
Kneeling and stealing is just so appealing
My fluid's potential forever your essential

Spinning around and around
You can always be found
In the hollows of my mind we're always entwined
Casting your gown, around on the ground
Leave nothing, oh nothing ever to be found

You are the artist; you know who you are,
Agog upon your easel
You are always a teasel

Arachne, arachne an outcast be you
Outcast, you out cast, upon the morning dew
So alluring your net, I can never forget
So perfect is the swell within your dell
Up and down and around on the ground
Weaving your web, ever tightening the thread

A silk for every occasion, needs little persuasion
Seamstress, temptress, dress and caress
Spin over limb with no needle or pin

Leashing the beast that you seek for your feast
Devouring, empowering, you like to control
Your feast is the beast that you never console

Silver web windows weep in the eye of October
Ever wonder, ever wonder, why I am not sober

Drunk in the face of lace upon the grain
Drunk in the face of lace upon the chase
Receptive is the line that just keeps on giving,
Giving and giving, unforgiving the living

There is no real fight
No return to flight, when all becomes night,
Its goodnight and goodnight.

134

Coarse and Ragged Shirt

I walk with thistle and gorse upon the mount of man,
I wear a coarse and ragged shirt.
I take refuge amongst the stones of abandoned belief,
I smell the salt spun upon the ocean's loom,
I hear the voices of a timeless womb,
I silently mouth a very old song,
A song sung before my birth and after my death,
When the herds of words have not diluted my breath.

About the Author

Greg Howes is a genealogist, writer and historical researcher based in Pembrokeshire, Wales, UK. Greg has lived in South West Wales for the last twenty-nine years, though he originates from Thame, Oxfordshire, England, UK.

Greg's work as a researcher has seen him present (and research for) family history programmes on television for both the BBC and ITV channels. He has taught family history (and horticulture, in his younger days) and featured on national and local radio stations, answering questions and giving advice on family history, the historical landscape and writing. This is Greg's fourth publication; he has written two novels, "The Man Behind the Glass" and "The Movement of Light," as well as a short illustrated Gothic romantic tale called "The Maidenswell Folly."He is also onboard the "Angel Shark Project: Wales," as an historical researcher of this rare and beautiful creature of the deep. Carew Castle also use Greg as an assistant on their night time Ghost and Historical tours. Greg is also a keen amateur lepidopterist.

He has written many articles for various magazines on subjects as diverse as local history, dating and archiving old photographs, and the history of woodland and ancient trees in the landscape.

His other pastimes include photographic art, archery, walking, swimming, watching motorcycle speedway and reading. His favourite authors include Arthur Conan Doyle, Arthur Machen, Peter Ackroyd, David Gemmell, Jack London, Charles Dickens, Bernard Cornwell, Algernon Blackwood, Henry Mayhew, Mary Stewart, Jack Vance, Robin Hobb, Edgar Allan Poe, Oliver Rackham, Charles Baudelaire, Marion Zimmer Bradley, Mary Shelley, H.P Lovecraft, Daphne Du Maurier, Bram Stoker, Sheridan Le Fanu, M.R James and Conn Iggulden.

His website can be found at -
www.welshfamilyhistory.co.uk

Facebook page -
https://www.facebook.com/GregHowesauthor/